To Live

and

Die in 1030

The Saga of Einar's Travels to the New World

Jorgen Flood

PublishAmerica
Baltimore

First printing

This is a work of fiction. Names, characters, places, and incidents either are the product of the author's imagination or are used fictitiously. Any resemblance to actual persons, living or dead, events, or locales is entirely coincidental.

PublishAmerica has allowed this work to remain exactly as the author intended, verbatim, without editorial input.

ISBN: 1-60563-252-X
PUBLISHED BY PUBLISHAMERICA, LLLP
www.publishamerica.com
Baltimore

Printed in the United States of America

Michael,

I hope you enjoy the book. Any similarity between you and any of characters is purely incidental and unintentional.

Jorgen

ACKNOWLEDGMENTS

This book would not have been possible but for the generous contribution of several friends and family members. In particular I would like to mention the following persons:

My wife, Susan, who has patiently accepted my late night writings and survived my sudden dashes to the PC, day or night. You have been supportive of (almost) all my ventures, including this one. Without your encouragement I would have stopped long ago.

Our good friends Paula Pierce and Dick Lolla have helped me tremendously with suggestions and editing. They were among the first to read the manuscript, and their positive comments, great ideas and Paula's editing skills have been instrumental in having this book published.

My Aunt Lita and her husband, Anders Ringnes, without whose support this book would never have happened.

My cousin Danielle Koren, whose drawings have made Einar come alive. She has made all the illustrations except for chapter 12. Danielle's fantastic drawings have adorned several books in Norway and I am deeply grateful that she took the time to help me with this project. The chapter 12 drawing is by Erik Flood.

Finally, I would like to say thank you to PublishAmerica for publishing my book.

To all of you, please accept my deepest appreciation for the work and time you have contributed to "Einar." It would not have happened without you.

TABLE OF CONTENTS

PREFACE: *Historical Notes on the Viking World* 9

CHAPTER 1: *Departure* 19

CHAPTER 2: *The Crossing* 34

CHAPTER 3: *The New Land* 54

CHAPTER 4: *The Maya* 70

CHAPTER 5: *The Retreat* 89

CHAPTER 6: *Fire* 98

CHAPTER 7: *The Trek* 104

CHAPTER 8: *The Old Camp* 122

CHAPTER 9: *A New Life* 142

CHAPTER 10: *A Freshwater Ocean* 165

CHAPTER 11: *The Canoe Trip* 173

CHAPTER 12: *Acceptance* 190

PRINCIPAL SOURCES AND RECOMMENDED READING 197

PREFACE

Historical Notes on the Viking World

The Viking world has fascinated writers and historians throughout the centuries. The "grandfather" of Norse mythology is Snorre Sturlason, who lived in Iceland from 1178 to 1241. He was an Icelandic historian, poet and politician, as well as the author of Heimskringla, a history of the Norwegian Kings, and other books. Ancient historians, like Snorre, were more partial and less historically accurate than modern historians strive to be. However, their dramatic style has an added value all of its own, beyond the strictly historical part. Snorre's history of the Norwegian Kings is still, in my mind, the ultimate story of the Viking age.

When I grew up in Norway during the 1950s and 1960s, the history of the Viking age was still largely based upon Snorre. My grandfather, an extremely vital and enthusiastic man, was the chief exponent in telling and dramatizing these stories to me. Though a pharmacist by profession, he loved the sagas, and few could retell the stories the way he did. He was easily the most influential person so far as my interest in history and adventure tales are concerned. His lively storytelling brought to life sword fights, holmgang (*two men set ashore on an island, from which only one escaped alive*), and far flung voyages to the distant corners of the earth. In my youthful imagination I was there, fighting alongside Olav Trygvason and Rollo, storming castles and cities, sword and shield in hand.

My grandfather certainly stimulated the artistic and creative genes not only in me, but also in his other grandchildren, and before that our parents. We are all avid readers today, and some have become very accomplished artists, as can be seen from the drawings in this book. Unfortunately, the kind of storytelling my grandfather practiced is unusual in these days of television and the internet.

What we today term the 'Viking Age' lasted from approximately 793 to 1066. Of course historical eras do not start or end at a particular time. They are a dynamic process. The timeline usually become obvious only long after the events took place. A case in point is World War II. Did it start in September 1939 with the attack on Poland, as we were told in school, or did it start the year before when Czechoslovakia was invaded? You could just as well argue that it started with Hitler's rise to power in 1933, or even use 1918 and the Treaty of Versailles as the starting point. Future historians may well choose a different interpretation from ours.

So also with the age of the Vikings. However, for practical purposes we tend to pick certain events symbolizing the beginning and the end of an era. For the Viking age, the raid on the Monastery of Lindisfarne in 793 usually marks the beginning. In 1066 King Harold of Essex, who had inherited the English throne, defeated the Norwegian King, Harald Hardrade, at Stamford Bridge. This battle often symbolizes the end of the Viking age. During that time span, the nature of the Viking onslaught changed dramatically. The initial raids were undertaken by a few ships, devastating monasteries, farms and villages. In the latter part of the period, large fleets, often commandeered by Scandinavian kings, were conquering lands and fighting to establish new kingdoms.

The roughly 250 years of the Vikings' rather dramatic entrance upon the world stage falls within the time period we call the early Middle Ages, and in many ways defines it. It was a time of religious fervor and marked the transition from antiquity to modern times. Populations grew fast and the cities in Europe were evolving rapidly. Sometimes unfairly described in the past as the "Dark Ages," we now see the Middle Ages as a period of considerable achievement and creativity. The Middle Ages also marked the beginning of the ascent of Europe as the world's powerhouse. For the people who lived in this period, though, it was not the Middle Ages. They felt they lived in modern times, just like us. They saw themselves as the most advanced societies on earth, the end product in the evolutionary chain. Christianity was the only true religion, and God protected them from heathen evils. The Vikings crushed this cozy image, and the societies of Europe had to react to them. A population will only allow itself to be raided so many times before countermeasures are found. By the time the raids faded, Europe was transformed, as was Scandinavia. Thereafter the Europeans themselves started looking outwards, exploring other parts of the world, first and most famously through the Crusades.

So who were these raiders and settlers from the North? Geographically they came from what we today call Scandinavia, i.e. Denmark, Norway and Sweden.

By European standards Scandinavia is a large area. Only Russia has a greater (European) landmass than Scandinavia, but Scandinavia was, and is, thinly populated. The three countries, and the settlements they created in Iceland and some of the smaller islands in the North Atlantic, share a common cultural heritage. Why the Northmen suddenly left their homeland and burst upon the world stage, however, is still debated. It was most likely caused by a combination of factors, including climatic changes, overpopulation, and opportunity.

Of course the will to raid is not enough, raiders also need a tool. The Longship, or Viking ship, provided this tool. It was, and still is, a magnificent vessel. The ingenuity of the Longship is in its versatility. The construction method (clinker built, i.e. one layer of wood partly overlapping the next) made it strong and flexible. This construction method is still in use for wooden pleasure boats in Scandinavia. The Longship could be sailed or rowed. Its sturdy construction allowed it to be used on the open ocean in all sorts of weather, yet its shallow draft also made it possible to go up rivers, or even pull it over land. Even today it is difficult not to be awed in the presence of the well preserved Longships displayed in Oslo and other places. A thousand years old, they still portray power and beauty.

In addition to exciting voyages, the word Viking conjures up images of wild warriors and even more violent behavior. "They came out of the North, like a bolt of lightening on an unsuspecting populace," is the way this saga starts. For the population of Medieval Europe it must have felt more like Armageddon than just a bolt of lightening. In fact they often saw it as punishment from God. In the churches the priests and the public prayed, "From the fury of the Northmen, Oh Lord deliver us." But the lord did not deliver them, at least not for several generations. But, were the Vikings really so cruel? Did they behave any worse than the Christians in their treatment of the Jews and Muslims, or later on the Indians? In my view they did not, though it is not my intention to whitewash their reputation. However, they did kill priests, monks and nuns, and to the Christians of the period that was the most incomprehensible of sins. Since the men who recorded history were mainly drawn from the clergy, they were for obvious reasons inclined to exaggerate the stories of Viking cruelty, making them into heathen monsters whenever they could. They did not to any large extent question the behavior of their own church and its members when they behaved likewise.

What about the Vikings as individuals, not the near mythical creatures of Snorre? What happened to them, the real men, those made of flesh and skin. What were they like? Our knowledge about them, and their era, has increased exponentially over the last few years. This is due to the use of modern DNA research, computer analysis and other scientific methods, all of which have given us a much deeper understanding of the past. The Vikings are no longer seen solely as a grey mass of bloodthirsty warriors, but also as individual men and women with dreams and aspirations, curiosity and greed, like men and women of all ages.

The Viking's exploits in navigation are legendary, and few dispute their far flung voyages to places like

Russia, Constantinople (Istanbul) and North America. Yet, there is still a perception that Leiv Eriksson's voyage to North America (Vineland) was a singular event. This is not the case. The Vikings established permanent settlements in New Foundland as well as Greenland, and the sagas tell of several journeys further south. How far did they go? We do not know, but probably quite far. Compared to crossing the Atlantic, voyages along the North American coastline must have been fairly easy. Besides, why should they behave differently than they did in other parts of the world? Why would they sail the rivers of Russia, but not those of North America?

That we have not yet found, and may never find, indisputable proof of their voyages beyond New Foundland is beside the point. Since they were not inclined to build stone castles or other large structures, few, if any, of their tools and artifacts would have survived a thousand years. How many ships sailed along the coast of North America? The sagas mention several expeditions, but of course many ship voyages were never documented. Numerous ships must have sailed in this period, and we can only guess how many disappeared. Many were lost at sea with all hands, but some may have met with adventures about which we can only guess.

A large part of this book deals with the American Indians. The Indians have been the subject of more scrutiny than the Vikings, and with less generous eyes. Historically, the treatment of their culture in books and movies was horrible, but fortunately it has gone from hostile and condescending to, more recently, understanding. Since history has always been written by the victors, the Indians have had a longer and harder fight for "justice" than most other peoples. Only towards the end of the 20th century did their culture receive the kind of praise its accomplishments and heritage so richly deserve. Again our knowledge about the time before Columbus is necessarily limited. By and large the Indians did not leave any written records, and with some notable exceptions, most of their structures were not the kind that would remain for later generations to see. In general the Indian tribes did not stay in one area, but relocated many times. Over the centuries considerable geographical changes took place. This was caused by pressure from more powerful tribes, changing weather patterns, and other events, natural and/or man made. However, our knowledge of the Indian world is also consistently advancing, and we have learnt many things about the pre Columbian world. For example, the bow and arrow were introduced around the period covered in this book. The other weapons described were also in use at this time. The geographical location of the Indian tribes should be generally correct, their customs as well.

The Maya empire was a vast and influential force in Central America and Mexico, and flourished at this time. Just like the Vikings, the Mayan's have a reputation for cruelty. Were they worse than their contemporaries, or for that matter the Europeans? Probably not, however cruel their rituals may seem by today's standards. Again, the written documentation is not delivered by the Mayan's themselves, but by their conquerors, who wanted to show the superiority of their own European beliefs and religion.

The other Central American tribe I mention is the Arawak. They had a complex social organization, but were not given to warfare. This was a key factor in their practical extinction at the hands of other Indian tribes, mainly the Carib, and later by the whites. Unfortunately for them, they inhabited much of the area where the early Europeans landed.

All the types of violence described in this book are documented in historical records, if not attributed to the specific tribe or place. I have purposely tried not to add violence just for the sake of violence. Yet this was in many instances a violent time, a time when moral constraints were very different from what we learn today. We cannot be too judgmental. Remember the violence present in our own time. The main difference is that today's tyrants may be held responsible at some point, and most modern religions discourage violence. Sadly though, considering what has recently happened in Yugoslavia, Rwanda and other places, that does not seem to be too much of a deterrent.

Finally, a few words regarding the Vineland saga as it developed after the time of this voyage. The trade in North American resources, via Iceland and Greenland, continued for a long time after 1030, with timber and other goods finding their way to Europe. The demise and disappearance of the Vineland and Greenland settlements, and the consequent loss of contact between the two worlds, changed the historical path. The end of the North American trade was caused by a combination of factors, including climatic changes and the Black Death among others. In general I believe the meeting of the two cultures,

European and Indian, could have been more amiable had the contacts continued. At least I would like to think so.

The lost contact paved the way for the later "re" discovery of the new world by Columbus, and the inability of the Indian peoples to resist the European onslaught. However, there are many indications that people in 1492 knew, or at least suspected, that there was land on the other side of the ocean. At the time many ship captains were also aware that the earth was round, regardless of what the church said. The knowledge of a land across the ocean had filtered down from Scandinavia, and the earlier Norse voyages.

Throughout this book I have tried to stay as close to history as possible. For practical reasons I have used the English names for Norse as well as Indian tribes and place names. The towns, tribes and places all existed, as did many of the characters mentioned. However, certain editorial liberties have been unavoidable, particularly in the last few chapters. Nevertheless, in the larger scheme of things, it is still my belief that this voyage could have taken place, and who knows, maybe it did!

CHAPTER 1

Departure

They came out of the North, like a bolt of lightning on an unsuspecting populace, fierce warriors from an unforgiving and even fiercer land. Their onslaught lasted only for about 250 years, roughly from 795 to 1066, but they left a giant footprint, one that speaks to us through the centuries. Their heathen gods set name to days and events, and many of their place names, like Normandy and Russia, are still with us today. The name by which they are known today is synonymous with adventure and terror. Yet behind the frightening façade they were men, individuals with dreams and fears like all men, trying to better their lot. That was of little comfort to those who stood in their way, brushed aside in one of the big sweeps of history.

They were the Vikings, warriors who took what they wanted with the sword, men with names like Harald Fairhair, Eirik Bloodaxe, Harald Bluetooth. Despite their bloody reputation, or rather because of it, they achieved the fame and immortality men have always craved, in a decidedly mortal time. To be remembered by coming generations was the ultimate goal, and to achieve that you had to do something memorable, or make a memorable case out of an ordinary event. Everybody knew the story of the king's man who pulled the arrow out of his chest, looked at the fat attached to it and said:

"The king has fed me well," then died. What a glorious way to perish!

Another immortal was the immensely strong archer, Einar Tambarskjelve, who fought for the famous warrior king, Olav Trygveson. His bow, combined with his strong arms, meant that his arrows could strike further than could any of his contemporaries'. In his last battle, an enemy arrow had snapped his bow in two.

"What snapped?" the king asked.

"Norway out your hand my King," Einar answered.

"It was not that loud," the king said, giving him his own bow. Einar Tambarskjelve pulled the king's bow back behind the head of the arrow, such was his strength.

"Too weak, too weak is the king's bow," he said.

For their contemporaries, these men achieved the ultimate goal: to be remembered for all time, an example to all men.

The tool that made Viking raids possible was the Longship, a beautiful vessel, long, slender and low. Yet it was also sinister and threatening, maybe because of the Dragon head at the bow, or perhaps due to its reputation. In the middle ages the Longship was in many ways the ultimate weapon, a doomsday machine for the oppressed and harassed peasants of Europe, already reeling under powerful lords and an almighty church.

* * * * * * * *

The ship that anchored in the harbor that day had none of that beauty, though. Its sails were in shreds, with blood spots and deep cuts in the woodwork from axes, swords and arrows. It looked sad, lost, anything but imposing and dauntless. For Einar Sigvaldsson and the others, the condition of this Longship was a sign, a warning, just as they were about to sail southward towards mainland Europe in their own attempt to win fortune and fame. In the year of the Lord 1030, to go Viking (raiding) in Europe gave you the opportunity to win both fame and fortune. In fact, it was the only way to win sudden riches and to honor one's family. To a Northman, family and reputation were everything. In a time before mass communication, to be remembered well was the most important of all. Yet, the sorry condition of this ship showed that raiding also provided opportunity for early death with little if any honor.

"They were all over us!" Skog exclaimed. "We killed many, but they kept coming. They are better organized than before, and their weaponry has improved. Worst of all they have Norse warriors fighting with them now." He spit on the ground. "Svear and Daner, mercenaries who live by killing their brethren. After six months of hardship we have less than when we left. Many families will go hungry this year."

As if to prove him right, women and children could be heard crying in the background as they looked in vain for their husbands or next of kin. They knew that without a provider they were reduced to begging, and beggars had a hard time surviving the harsh Scandinavian winter.

Einar didn't say anything in response. He looked down at his own ship. It was beautiful, quite a contrast, with its dark wood finish, unblemished hull and clean sails. It was twenty-four meters (eighty feet) long, seven meters (twenty-three feet) wide and weighed in at about twelve tons. It normally carried thirty oarsmen. Einar pondered what he should do if raiding in Europe was no longer a good prospect. He had to leave Norway. His family had sided with the disposed king, Olav Haraldsson (later to be known as Saint Olav), and powerful families had put a price on his and his brother's heads. The homestead had been stolen from them by wealthy chieftains on the winning side. Not only did they have no home to return to, but he was the only one left. His brother rested in a shallow grave, thrown in like a bag of potatoes after the battle. At least that was what he had been told. Einar got angry thinking about it. He wanted to bury his family like chieftains, but now it was impossible. Winning was everything, and they had lost.

It had started so well. Olav had been victorious for many years, but the alliance of powerful Norwegian chieftains (Jarls) and the mighty Danish King, Knut the Great, had been too much even for Olav. His efforts to force Christianity on the country through the "take it or die" method, as Einar silently called it, created too many enemies. Einar, although accustomed to violence like most people of his time, did not agree with Olav's methods. They created resentment among the free farmers and other groups. To Einar, violence should only be used when it served a purpose.

Einar had let himself be baptized, partly because Olav demanded it, but mainly out of convenience. He was not a very religious man, but the old gods certainly did not make much sense to him. They were too much like men, not godlike at all, drinking and womanizing as much as they wanted. Maybe it was time to try something different. The new Christian god apparently had some human traits too—after all he had a son! Einar had heard the stories regarding King Olav's body after the battle, how his nails and hair had continued to grow, and other miracles. Many Christians took this as proof of Olav's divinity, that he was favored by the Christian god. For his own sake, Einar did not attach much credence to these stories. Olav was pretty earthly in his view, and certainly not very saintly in the way he treated others, but Einar noticed how people often changed their perception about a person once he was dead.

What to do! Two years ago, Einar and his brother had raided in Europe, and though they were successful, the pay-off was not anywhere near what they had expected. He also realized he did not like raiding that much. He had no moral qualms (he would not have understood the word) but rather a pity for some of their victims. The terror in their eyes, which many found amusing, made him feel uncomfortable, though he was careful not to say so, or to show it. That would have invited ridicule and endless jokes at his expense, not something a Viking cherished. One Viking had made a disreputable name for himself when he refused to participate in a game of "catching small children on a spear." He was for ever after known as "Barnekjær" (child-lover), an ignoble stamp for a warrior.

There was another reason for Einar's uncertainty about raiding in Europe. Though he could not put a finger on it, and certainly would not have understood it fully, times were changing and the age of the Vikings was coming to an end. In fact the days of the small raids were already long gone. Only whole fleets and not individual ships were now able to overcome the defenses built by the villages and towns of Europe. Einar did not view Skog as a great warrior, yet he was no dope either, and what had happened to Skog could easily happen to him. He looked around the small town with its longhouse, small houses and surrounding farms. Against the towering West Coast mountains of Norway the beauty was undeniable, yet it was a brutal beauty, framed in by harsh winters, and unreliable short summers.

What to do? Where to go? When Einar was young

the town seemed big, but now that he had seen some of the big cities in Europe it seemed small and poor with its 150 to 200 odd houses. Its streets were filled with garbage and dirt, with planked walks between the houses and full of people and animals scurrying about. In fact most things that had so impressed him as a little boy now seemed poor and dirty. Even the community long house with its 90 foot length seemed small compared to what could be seen on the continent. However, the town still had a certain attraction, since its houses created a unity, a commonness of purpose. The very first time he came to a town, his father had told him about city life, how the laws had established standards for what could be called a city dwelling. According to his father, a city house had to have at least three rooms, one of which was used for animals and food storage. In fact the towns were in many ways just a number of farms clustered together. Einar cherished the memories of his travels with his father, and how he had always taken time to answer Einar's myriads of questions. In fact both his parents, Sigvald and Torgunn, had been fair and level headed, not very strict by the standards of the day. He and his brother had been loved by both, and since it was only the two of them (his mother could not have any more children after she got violently sick and aborted during her third pregnancy) they received more attention than did children in the normally much larger families of 1030.

Einar was a powerfully built man, dark-haired with penetrating blue eyes. At five feet, ten inches he was slightly taller than average for his time, but there were many taller warriors around. Since most

Scandinavians were several inches taller than their European contemporaries, undoubtedly a fact that had enhanced their fearsome reputation, Einar felt big while raiding. His father had been an expert with the axe, and his instructions combined with Einar's good physique meant that Einar was now known to be an expert with all the most usual weapons, axe, spear and sword. Few men would want to confront him in battle unless supported by others.

Enough daydreaming! He knew he had to make a decision. His thirty-two man crew expected it. Several of them had to leave the country as well. Originally they had planned to settle somewhere in Europe, but now that did not seem so tempting. They had heard stories of great religious anger towards the Northmen, anger that made it difficult for a Northman to live safely outside Scandinavia. The Christian church, which is where the stories of the time were written, had made monsters out of the Northmen. But in more than one of the cities they had stormed, they had found instruments of torture well beyond what the Northmen used. Not only that, they often found people who had obviously been tortured for extended periods. Einar particularly remembered a castle where they found a girl whose limbs were quite useless as all the ligaments and joints had been twisted around. She was quite mad by the time they came, so they killed her. There was nothing they could do to help her anyway. Though often cruel, the Vikings were more spontaneous, and they did not take the time to create elaborate torture instruments.

Einar looked around the harbor again. Something

he had heard rattled his mind. What was it? Something about another lawless man, that was it, his name was Eirik the Red. Suddenly he remembered—Eirik had sailed west from Iceland and found new land, Greenland. One of his sons, Leiv, had sailed even further west and discovered another new island. The stories told of a land green and rich, with large animals and mighty trees. That was it, he made the decision right there and then. 'We will sail west to Iceland and beyond,' he said to himself. They knew they could not settle in Iceland or Greenland, since his allegiance to King Olav and the new faith was well known, and the allegiance of many Icelandic families were to the old ways, Though not personal enemies, he knew the long arm of the Danish king could easily reach him even in Iceland or Greenland, and the Icelandic chieftains would certainly not support a Norwegian Christian.

The decision lifted a burden off his shoulders and he announced the plan to his crew and friends. Nine of them refused to go and there was little he could do. They were free men, and unlike in continental Europe with its vast stock of farmers tied to their lord and land in almost slave-like obedience, the Northmen valued their freedom. The Scandinavian chieftains never had the same power over the life of their subjects that the European clergymen and lords had, and would still have for a few more centuries. The Northern lands were too vast and the populations too small. The harsh climate did not allow the farmers to produce the kind of agricultural surpluses that would allow lords and clergymen a life of idle luxury, or endless military adventures.

The rest of Einar's crew, though a little disappointed, accepted the decision. After all, what had happened to Skog was a warning to them as well. The places of the nine who refused to go were rapidly filled. Strangely enough, two of the new crew were single women, women who had lost their fathers or husbands on Skog's trip. Einar was a little uneasy about bringing women. True, they were not primarily out to raid, but seven women (including two female trells, or slaves) among twenty-seven men could easily cause jealousies and other trouble. Besides, they were not so strong at the oars. Eight of his crew were originally Svear, but family problems made it difficult for them to go back to Sweden. After some contemplation he decided to take them all, Swedes and women included—who knew what they might find or need?

With the decision made to sail west, things were set in motion. Supplies were carried aboard, dried fish, salted meat, extra wood, things that would be needed. There was a certain excitement in the air, something that naturally follows when men know that they are about to venture into the unknown.

Many of his crew had mixed feelings though. Espen did not like the switch to a westward voyage. In order to help his family out of a difficult financial situation, he had sworn to the relatives of Tore Hund, one of King Olav's principal enemies, that he would kill Einar. That would have been easier during a big battle in Europe than during a small skirmish in the western islands. Yet he did not have much choice. Honor to himself and his family demanded that he try.

Using Holmgang was out of the question. Espen had seen Einar with axe and sword, and knew he would not last long in a fight. There was another reason Espen had to complete his mission. He had heard rumors that another man had been sent to kill him as well as Einar if he failed or did not try. Was the other assassin among the crew as well?

Gisle was happy about the impending departure. Born as the youngest son in a particularly brutal family, he had always been at the receiving end of blows and abuse. His whole life had one guiding star: how to avoid beatings and punishment. At twelve he had become a master at blending into the surroundings, and at fifteen he usually managed to make others take the blame for things he did, but not always. At twenty-two he had grown very strong and was mostly left alone. He could easily have beaten up his father by then, but no son could beat up his father in 1030 without severe retaliation, and his father had helpers. Not only was his father, and older brothers, physically brutal, they also lacked any compassion for others, even his mother and other family members. It was a world of almost total selfishness, each man for himself. Gisle knew that the day his father died, he and his brothers would immediately start fighting over the farm. Nobody would want to share even a minor part of the inheritance. His mother had died many years ago, mostly from abuse, but also from a broken heart following the early death of her only daughter. In fact, his sister had been the only happy person in the whole family as far as Gisle was concerned. Her death had marked the end of any kind of family atmosphere for Gisle. His father and brothers on the other hand, had not even bothered to stay home the day of the funeral; they had just gone a little later to the local tavern. How to avoid punishment and abuse! To do that, anywhere except his father's farm seemed a good place to be.

Gunhild did not want to go on this trip, but she had to. There were many strong, independent and powerful women in medieval Norway, but Gunhild was not among them. Her husband had always dreamed of winning wealth and fortune on a Viking raid, and she had to follow him on this trip. Her family was poor, and when their slightly wealthier neighbor, Geir, decided he needed a wife, her parents agreed to provide Gunhild to him immediately. One less mouth to feed was their only thought. Despite all, she wasn't too unhappy. Geir was not a dream date, but he was much better than her almost continually drunk father and brothers, and the hopeless poverty and brutality that followed. At least he did not beat her, nor did he drink more than was customary. Her mother, who had once been a very pretty girl according to local gossip, was now but a drunken witch, making a fool of herself and everybody around her. When a cousin had raped her at a young age, Gunhild's family was basically paid off in booze. With a stronger (and she was thinking sober) family it would have ended in blood or large payoffs. And to think they should have been reasonable well off. The farm could have provided for all of them if properly tended, but it was not to be. After her marriage, and improved material conditions, the memory of the poverty of her early years nevertheless stayed with her. She was always careful about sharing her food and valuables, hiding bits and pieces everywhere. One less mouth to feed! She was determined not to be that hungry mouth if something happened to Geir and she was left alone. They had only been married for a year, and had no children yet. To stay behind in Norway would mean moving back to her family, and she would rather go on a raid than do that.

Leone was a trell, one of only three in the crew. The other trells were Thorfast and Oddny. Slavery was not unknown, but neither was it widespread in Scandinavia. Trelldom was not quite as bad as slavery in antiquity, but not that much better. Leone had been captured and carried away as a young girl from her village in Germania. She did not remember much from her previous life, but remembered vividly the beginning of her captivity. The foul smell of the men, the language she did not understand, the strange food, the intense discomfort on the wet and cold boat, it was all burnt into her memories. Another memorable event was the intense cold of her first Nordic winter. It seemed to last forever, and even the sun was deceiving, just a cold circle in the sky with no heat. She had to sleep in the barn with the animals, but that was actually the best part of her captivity. At least the animals did not bother her. Her master, Olav, who had purchased her from the raiders to help on the farm, would come out for her occasionally, but at least it did not last long and she had not become pregnant. At least Olav was not cruel. He demanded obedience and plenty of work, but was rarely hitting her. To book passage on the ship, Olav had pretty much used her as payment and a bargaining chip in his negotiations with Einar, offering her services as a cook, to mend clothes and other women's work. She was a little afraid of Einar, fearing that he might be worse than Olav. The devil known is better than the one not known. As it was Einar had blue sympathetic eyes, and he never touched Leone or beat her. At times she was wondering if he had noticed her at all. Still, Leone's days were long and hard. Life in the 11th century was hard under all circumstances, but in a time steeped in tradition, family and religion, one accepted one's lot or died. Leone accepted her lot, though at times she felt protest, anger, resentment, and hate. But it was all to no avail—what could she do? The hardest part was not really having anybody to talk to. Oddny was older than Leone and did not say much. Her spirit was broken, and she did not harbor any hope for the future. She was just a shell living one day after another. It was impossible not to feel sorry for her, a life wasted in misery.

Thorfast was difficult to talk to as well. He was bitter, the way poor people get when they feel they have been dealt an unfair hand and betrayed. Thorfast was what in later centuries would be known as a Prisoner of War, but his family could not, or maybe would not, pay for his release. There were many children in his family to feed, and his parents, if they were still around, probably did not make too much of an effort to learn about his whereabouts. Either way his home near Jorvik in present day England was now a distant memory. In England he had been the son of a free farmer, not wealthy maybe, but still it was difficult for him to adjust to being a slave. He had never really heard or seen the Viking raiders. It had all happened so fast. He was on his way to visit a local girl when they had caught him. Clubbed to the ground almost immediately, he woke up in the Longship just as it departed for Norway. His only hope was escape, but how? One had to use a ship to get to England. Dark and five foot, four inches, he did not look Nordic, and would be caught swiftly. Maybe this trip would offer him a chance to get out of trelldom.

The rest of the crew did not care too much where they went. For various reasons they had to leave, and this was a way to win fame and fortune, or nothing. The alternative was to stay in Norway, facing another winter with little work and almost certain starvation. Only the gods knew what lay ahead, but the gods were secretive as always, talking only when it pleased them.

CHAPTER 2
The Crossing

Three days later they set sail. It was early spring and the weather was good. Like many of his contemporaries, Einar was a master sailor and navigator. The trip from Norway to Iceland was the longest open sea voyage he and his crew would encounter on this trip. It was, however, well known to Norse seafarers since the Icelandic trade was fairly active by the standards of the day. The boat was crowded with supplies and crew, but not more than was usual on trips of this sort. After two days, they encountered a small storm. It was nothing like the dreaded winter storms, yet rough enough in a small open ship. At one point of the storm, as the ship practically surfed down a large wave, Oddny lost her balance and fell down towards the rear tiller, picking up speed on the slippery woodwork. As she careened into the side of the boat with a thud, she tried to grab hold of one of the ropes, but did not manage to hold on and was thrown ten feet clear of the boat, disappearing into the waves almost immediately. It all happened so fast nobody really had time to react. Though Einar was annoyed at the loss, he decided against going back to look for her. It would have taken too much time, and she was in her late thirties, too old to be valuable. The odds of finding her alive were slim anyway. This was their only mishap on the way to Iceland, and Oddny was a trell of little consequence.

Leone was sad to see her go. They were not friends as such, but her fellow trell's disappearance meant more work for her and Thorfast, who acted as cook. Leone wondered if Oddny had fallen overboard, or simply lost the will to live and finally found a way out of her misery. Leone thought it was an accident, and Oddny's frightened face as she tumbled overboard stayed with her for several days, but she was never completely sure. The loss of Oddny also meant there was a little more space for her to sleep so it was not all bad.

The Longship was truly a small boat on a vast ocean. To the casual observer it looked like it was too small, the freeboard was too low, and there was no cabin to shield the crew from the elements. But the casual observer would have been wrong. The Longship was a marvel of 10th century engineering. Its shallow draft allowed it to go up rivers for trade, or raiding, and when necessary, to escape more powerful warships. It could be rowed or sailed, even pulled over land. For hundreds of years these elegant vessels crossed the world's oceans, giving their crews unparalleled mobility at a time when the majority of the world's inhabitants never ventured more than a few miles from home.

But Einar and his crew saw none of these qualities. It wasn't that they did not know of them, they just took them for granted. At a time when technological changes came slowly, the Longships had always been there, at least from their perspective, and the time before they were born they knew little about. What they did know was mainly from folk tales and tall stories. They had complete faith in their vessel, and were confident that no matter what happened, they would be ready.

Since this would be a long voyage, the crew had stocked up primarily on dried meat, fish, butter and a drink made from sour milk that lasted a long time. If room allowed it they would have brought live animals, like sheep, to provide fresh meat. However, Einar had decided against it on this particular voyage, saving the space for men and weapons. Thorfast acted as the cook (usually it was a trell or man of low birth) and he was responsible for bringing enough food. Beatings were usually the punishment if the cook failed in this duty. Fresh fish and shore raids (strandhogg) could supplement the stock of food and supplies, and if time permitted they could even do some hunting.

They were well armed for their time. Each man carried his own weapons and armor. Most were armed with axes, some with swords and spears. For protection they had helmets and shields, and a lucky few had chain-mail and various leather patches. The shields were usually made out of wood, often with a metal band and/or a metal core to strengthen them. They also had smaller weapons like knives and daggers. The clothes and armor had few if any ornaments since these would have been a liability in combat. The weapons were a mix of many types and had often been taken from fallen enemies, which meant they carried weapons from various European countries as well as the Near East and Byzantium.

As the days passed by Einar had plenty of time to think. Most of all his thoughts wandered to the battle of Stiklestad a year earlier. He could never finish with that, and spent hours reminiscing about it with Geir who had also been there. It had been a mighty battle, one to tell their children about. For Geir, it had been just that, a big glorious battle. For Einar it was more, a watershed, a point in time which would shape the rest of his life. The bloodletting was enormous by Norwegian standards, yet it was also magnificent to look back at the battle, the gleaming swords and shields, the battle cries, the moaning of the wounded and dying. Einar had been part of the force facing Tore Hund and Torstein Knarresmed (Torstein Shipbuilder), a man King Olav had previously punished for murder by taking away one of his new trading ships. When the alliance to overthrow King Olav had come together, Torstein had seen his chance for revenge. He approached Tore Hund saying he wanted to fight with him. Tore and his men accepted Torstein and his men as one of their own. Tore and Torstein's battle cry had been "Forward, forward farmers!" while Einar and the rest of the King's men had answered "Forward, forward Christ's men, King's men!"

Initially the battle had gone well for Olav and his men. Due to some misunderstandings, the opposition had even shot arrows at each other. As in all civil wars, it was difficult to distinguish friend and foe. But Olav's advantage did not last. The king's men were vastly outnumbered, and within a short time the opposition's strength in numbers started to show. It was a powerful battle, and the king himself fought hard. In the end, the king faced Tore Hund directly, and while fighting him, one of Tore Hund's men cut Olav down. After the king fell, his force disintegrated. It is usual in battles for the heaviest losses to occur when one army is fleeing the battlefield and Stiklestad was no different. As Olav's lines crumbled, the rear echelons turned and fled. The panic spread, and more and more of the king's men were cut down as they tried to do the same.

Einar was in the middle of some of the hardest fighting, and upon seeing the King killed, was beginning to accept that he would probably die there. He was exhausted from fighting and killing, nauseous from the smell of death and blood. He tried to move out of the front line, but his legs could barely carry him. Just when all hope seemed to be lost, he saw a possible escape. A herd of maybe thirty horses was standing behind the enemy line, waiting for their owners to come back after the fight. Cavalry was little used in Scandinavia. Horses were mainly seen as a means for transportation, and of course they were difficult to bring on ships where they demanded too much space and supplies. If Einar and his men could break through the lines, they could take the horses and make a run for it. Quickly he told the men closest to him his plan. They nodded and, gathering their remaining strength, dashed forward screaming at the top of their lungs. It was a complete surprise to the enemy who had come to believe victory was theirs and expected only to be pursuing and cutting down frightened fleeing men. With surprising ease, Einar's small band of maybe twenty men broke through and charged toward the horses. They had only two-hundred feet to go, then one-hundred feet. Some of the enemy recognized what was happening and turned after them, but it was too late. One of the enemy warriors who protected the horses lifted his sword in defiance as Einar and the others came charging towards him. His first stroke cut Einar's sword in two, but despite this he did not have a chance against this group of desperate men. Einar threw the sword stump away and, as he caught the warrior's next blow on his shield where it got stuck in the wood center portion, he pulled his knife and stabbed the enemy. He could feel the knife cutting flesh, the life essence of the other man shivering on the sharp blade. Einar took his enemy's sword, and continued without hesitation toward the horses. The whole incident had taken but a few minutes.

The remaining horse tenders, most just being older boys with little warrior experience, were quickly killed or chased away. Einar and his men grabbed the horses and rode off. He felt like a man reborn, enthralled by the elation of the escape, the wind blowing in his face. He cried out a final:

"Long live the king!"—A rather odd phrase when he thought about it later since the king had just been killed—and felt as if he flew from the battlefield thrilled to be alive.

When they realized nobody was following them, they slowed down. The enemy probably had enough loot and prisoners as it was to worry about a small band like theirs. Einar looked at the sword he had taken. It was the nicest weapon he had ever seen. The blade was thirty inches long and two inches wide, straight but with a pointed end. It had a bluish color, and the iron was much sharper and stronger than he was used to. The handle was twelve inches long of a hard treated wood, and since it was also much lighter than a Norseman would expect, the sword could be used with either one or two hands. Einar concluded it had to be from the Mediterranean area, maybe from Miklagard (Constantinople) or some other southern city. Workmanship like this did simply not exist in Scandinavia. For the rest of his life the sword accompanied Einar. He kept it well greased, and never tired of looking at the beautiful workmanship.

Despite their almost miraculous escape, the aftermath of battle was a sad turning point for the small group of survivors. Einar had initially gone back to the farm, where he learned about his brother's fate, but was soon informed of a powerful group of warriors coming for him and his farm. He knew further fighting would be a lost cause, so before they arrived he rode down to the nearest coastal town with his fellow survivors. His family had a Longship there, and by sailing around the Norwegian coast, he had escaped. In addition to losing their land, they had also lost their king and many friends.

Einar did not have any regrets about the Stiklestad battle and the killing of so many men in the modern sense of the word, implying moral judgment or distinguishing right from wrong, but he felt it was a terrible waste of Norwegian men and resources. The battle was a disaster. Those who sided with the Danish king, Knut the Great, had done it for good reasons. They wanted to be completely free and self-governed, but in the end all they did was weaken Norway as a nation, exchanging a Norwegian king for domination by Denmark. After the battle, the manpower was simply not there to maintain full independence. Norway, with its hundreds of small isolated valleys and fjords, always had difficulty raising large armies, and now a huge portion of the available manpower had been wasted in a civil war. It had all been so unnecessary. If Olav had been a bit less fanatical with regard to his religion, the grand alliance against him would not have been so powerful. But there was something else as well. The battle was a break with the past, the beginning of the end of an era. The peoples of Europe had learned well from their tormenters and were now better organized, better able to resist the Nordic onslaught. Monks and priests had arrived in Scandinavia and were turning people to Christianity. The old gods, Odin and Tor, were tired and lost their powers as the old ways started to disappear. Though victorious in the battle, it was as if Stiklestad was their last victory, a pyrrhic one.

"Land O Hoi!" Einar was shaken out of his

daydreaming. This was a new beginning for them, a new land, with new opportunities for wealth or more death. A single seagull hung over the ship. 'Why only one?' Einar wondered, 'there should be a dozen or so.' One was a bad sign, almost an omen that one ship alone was at the mercy of the new God, or was it the old northern Gods. He could not completely give up his old beliefs; after all it was better to stay on a good footing with all gods, just in case he was wrong.

With the help of the stars, the sun and a translucent stone, they made good time. The translucent stone was used when it was overcast to determine where the sun was. It glowed on the side facing the sun. In addition to the stone they had a sundial. With just these basic tools, Einar and other seafarers were able to navigate the oceans with remarkable accuracy.

They were greeted in Hjardarholt on Iceland in a justifiably cautious, if not unfriendly, way. Einar was known even there as a fierce warrior and one of King Olav's chieftains. He was not one to cross without good reason. The conspicuous crew's plan was to stay in Iceland for a couple of weeks to replenish the ship, but fate intervened. Einar first enjoyed seeing Hjardarholt, different as it was from Norway. Though it was in many ways a typical medieval village, the houses where constructed differently due to the shortness of timber on Iceland. The extra use of mud and stone made them even darker than in the rest of Scandinavia, and after a while the whole place seemed gloomy to him. Einar decided it was not a place he wanted to stay longer than necessary. This was his first visit to Iceland, and he met up with Thor, an old comrade in arms from King Olav's army. Thor, a huge six foot three inches tall man, with a voice to go with his big frame, took him to a place where warm water came out of the ground. Einar had heard about such places, but never seen them before. He wondered aloud why the water came up like that

"It is warmed by the volcanoes, the liquid fire under the ground." Thor said. As they were sitting in the heated natural pool, two young women came and started to massage their necks and backs, a very comfortable experience Einar decided.

"You could stay here, Einar," Thor said. "Iceland needs warriors. We will help you against your enemies"

"If Knut or some of his allies come, they will have too many ships for us to fight," Einar said, "but that is unlikely. I heard rumors that he will sail towards Sweden. There is much more wealth there, and he also has England to think about."

Thor was quiet for a while.

"You are probably right," he said, "but why not stay here anyway? I doubt there is much to win in the Western islands All we seem to get from Greenland and Vineland is fish, meat, grapes, timber and the like. I have not seen any gold or other valuables."

"I have heard stories of vast wealth further south," Einar said.

"Bah, just tall tales, wild stories among so many others. Mark my word, nothing good will come out of your voyage. Here you can be a big man; we can rule Hjardarholt between us."

'So there it is', Einar thought, 'Thor wants an ally to win power for himself. I will be drawn into another war, exactly what I don't need right now. Besides Hjardarholt is not a prize worth all that fighting.' But these were not thoughts he could say out loud.

"Maybe when I come back,' he said instead, "but for now my crew expects to see the Western lands. There may not be any riches there, but stories come from somewhere, and it may be worthwhile to see for oneself." He was certain that upon his return things would be different anyway.

Their third day in Iceland, Einar, Ulf and many of the others spent time drinking with Thor and some of his men in the meetinghouse. Ulf, one of Einar's old friends among the crew, was usually a quiet man, but he became difficult when drunk. Initially the mood was good, and the beer even better.

"It is amazing how easy beer goes down after days at sea," Thor said. Most of the men stated their agreement. Looking around, Einar saw the house was typically Norse in construction, with no windows but with small holes in the walls that created an almost surreal atmosphere. Children and animals ran around chasing mice and rats in the corners. Einar gazed at one of the girls there. What could be seen of her legs were long and slender and her hair, in two braids, framed a pretty face, even if her mouth was a bit too wide. Einar was not the only one trying to get her attention, but the looks she threw him were inviting. He smiled at a distant memory and concentrated on the beer. Womanizing was definitely not what he had come for, but there was no denying the pressure he felt when he was looking at her.

Two men in the corner argued over the game they were playing and grew louder and louder. Einar realized one of them was Ulf, while the other was an Icelander unknown to him. Both were obviously drunk, and the argument suddenly turned ugly before anybody could intervene. Punches were thrown and insults hurled. It was clear from his friends' shouts that the Icelander's name was Odd Quickdrop. The argument was tremendously heated and, despite the fact that both men were drunk, such personal attacks could only be settled one way. Normally Einar did not mind his men fighting others, winning glory for themselves and the ship, but these were not ordinary times and he needed a complete crew. This visit to Iceland was definitely not the place or time to risk losing a life. But Ulf was a free man and there was nothing Einar could do to stop the ensuing course of events. He had to watch as the ground outside the longhouse was cleared for a contest of principle.

People came from far away to see the fight. A duel between two obviously skilful warriors was not something that could be seen every day, and the fact that they came from two different places added to the excitement. Ulf was the bigger and stronger looking man, and most bets went in his favor. Sobering up by the time the fight started, he regretted his actions, but he could not say so, nor could he withdraw from the fight with honor intact. Both men lined up and pulled their weapons, both had powerful battle axes with wood handles, but there the likeness stopped. Ulf's axe was double sided, while Odd's had just one sharp end. That made it lighter, but you also had to be more careful with how you held it. Geir and Einar discussed which was the better weapon.

"I prefer the double sided," Geir said. "Sure it is

heavier, but that also means it is not so easily deflected by a shield or armor".

Einar disagreed. He felt the lighter weight would not tire Ulf so fast, and he could be quicker with blows and thrusts. In addition to their axes, both men had helmets and wood shields with a metal outer ring.

Ulf drew first blood with his axe, as he almost split Odd's shield in half, cutting off one of Odd's fingers in the process. A murmur went through the spectators, most agreeing that the shield must have been poorly made to split so easily. Odd's return blow hit Ulf's side, which started to bleed, but the chain mail saved his life this time. Both men wounded, they grew careful, trading blows while protecting themselves with their shields, or in Odd's case with what was left of it. Ulf backed away from Odd's quick cuts and thrusts, and now they all knew where his last name came from. Einar had never seen anybody cutting or thrusting his weapon with such speed, and for the first time felt uneasy about the outcome, even if the battle somehow vindicated his opinion about the two axe types. The strain of battle made both men sweat profusely, and the stench of sweat and blood made everybody eerily quiet. Nothing could be heard except the sound of weapons and grunts from the combatants. Suddenly Ulf stumbled over a branch and fell backwards. Odd was on him like a tiger, his axe almost cutting Ulf's head down the middle, but not before Ulf's final thrust went through Odd's chain mail and into his stomach. It was over for both men, Ulf died immediately, while Odd shook violently on the ground. His family ran over to him, holding him down, comforting him, but nothing could really be done, except casting hateful glances towards Einar's men. The whole audience started talking almost as if on command, and there was general agreement it had been a glorious fight. However, with Ulf dead and his opponent dying, Einar knew his crew would have to leave as soon as possible. He did not want to be drawn into any more family feuds.

Both Gunhild and Leone had watched the fight.

"I don't like it," Gunhild whispered mostly to herself. "Why do men have to fight and die over such silly things?"

To her surprise Leone answered;

"They don't have enough to do. All they think about is glory and their own silly pride, they're just like little boys fighting over a toy." She looked at Gunhild a little scared, knowing she could be beaten for speaking out of line to a free woman. The words just came out of her before she could think. Gunhild just smiled.

"I could not have said it better myself," she said.

Despite their difference in rank, that of a free woman versus a trell, she found she liked Leone, and in any case she was not one to enjoy anybody being beaten, particularly not somebody who had been dealt an even harsher lot in life than herself. Then both girls realized Einar was right behind them, and he had obviously heard what they said. He did not change his facial expression, but Gunhild thought she saw a twinkle in his eye. In any event he just walked away, not to be bothered by women talk. Leone looked frightened, a trell could be punished for so many things,

"Don't' worry Leone, he is not one to talk around," Gunhild laughed, she well understood Leone's predicament. Nevertheless both girls felt relieved that he ignored their whole conversation.

To avoid further unnecessary problems and revenge killings, Thor recommended to Einar that they leave as soon as possible. Einar ordered two men continuously on guard in the ship, sober and with weapons ready. The whole crew, save for the women and slaves would take guard turns of four hours each. While in town, none of his men would walk alone, but should be in groups of three or more at all time. The precautions worked. No more trouble ensued during their stay in Iceland. They traded for supplies and after four more days, with the ship replenished and ready, continued west. This time their goal was Greenland, and since it was still summer, they had pleasant sailing. Einar and the rest of the crew were awed by Greenland's wild countryside and deep fjords, framed by magnificent glaciers in the background. With no trees and a barren landscape, it still had majestic beauty. The name "Green" seemed to be a misnomer though. It was probably named to make it sound more attractive than it really was. A trick used to make it more attractive to settlers. At one place they saw a large piece of glacier splitting off, thundering into the ocean, creating a large wave. The clear cool air and deep blue waters with the glaciers in the background formed a picture of perfect isolation and splendor at the same time.

They did some fishing and minor hunting for seals and birds, but had been told in Iceland that polar-bear hunting was the king of sports. For several days all the men did was looking for polar bears. As they passed a small glacier at the entrance of a small fjord, they finally saw a bear and several men jumped ashore to chase it. This was life! They were all excited, expecting a juicy steak for dinner. But as fate would have it, they went ashore between the bear and its cub, and consequently the mother bear did not try to run away. As they approached, it got up on its hind legs and roared. They realized they were facing one of the biggest living predators on earth, and it was much bigger than they had thought, much bigger than it had appeared from the ship. The hunting plan suddenly did not look so good anymore. Emitting another ear-splitting roar, the bear came straight toward them with surprising speed. Men who a second earlier had been preparing for a kill now clamored to get out of its way. Espen felt as if ice was running through his veins. He tried to jump out of the way, but his legs just would not move. Luckily for him the bear raced past him about six feet away. Not being fast enough, two of the men who were right in front of the cub were thrown to the side as the mother bear charged through their line, not stopping to fight but aiming straight for the sea. Her cub followed her into the water.

After a stunned silence, somebody called out, asking if anybody were missing. They had been lucky, nobody had been seriously hurt. The two men the bear had pushed to the side emerged with only minor scratches and cuts.

"Well, the two of you do not look any better than you did before, but it looks like we will not get polar bear steaks today," Espen said, feeling smug with himself for hiding his embarrassing performance with a joke. They all laughed, as much from the comment as from their own miserable behavior. However, a seal was captured a few hours later and prepared soon afterwards. The meat was good tasting and nourishing.

Scandinavian winters had prepared them for the cold. 'There is no such thing as a bad day, only bad clothes!' was their refrain. Since the weather held up they enjoyed the sailing. Even the trells who were usually too tired to really enjoy the scenery marveled at the shifting colors in the ice, the white glaciers and deep blue ocean. But beauty was not what they had come for, and while cruising around the cold fjords, they decided to continue directly west as soon as possible. The Greenlanders living in Brattalid, their stop in Greenland, recommended they bypass Helluland (Baffinland) on their way west, heading directly for Vineland. Brattalid was another barren settlement, and as with Hjardarholt, Einar could not see why anybody would live in such a small isolated place. Nevertheless they enjoyed their stay. The Greenlanders obviously loved to have visitors and much mjoed (beer) was consumed while stories from Scandinavia were told and retold. This time however, Einar had decided to stay sober and stop any trouble before it started. In fact, he said that if anybody got into any sort of fights they would be left behind. The threat had the desired effect, and they enjoyed their short time there, the whole crew staying in line. One of the Greenlanders tried to purchase Leone, and for a time Einar was afraid another fight would be brewing despite his precautions. Fortunately he managed to joke the whole incident away, telling how much they would miss Leone's cooking. Leone was incredibly relieved when the whole affair was settled without any transaction. Spending the rest of her life in this cold climate did not appeal to her at all.

Two weeks after departing Greenland they came upon the small settlement in Vineland (New Foundland) where they spent some time talking to the local villagers. It was a desolate place, an outpost of Scandinavian civilization such as it was, but not a place that had any attraction to Einar. He had seen the cities and lands of Europe, and this cold and lonely place was a complete turn-off to him. Even Brattalid and Hjardarholt seemed like hives of activity compared to this place. The wind swept over the land, with few trees or bushes to provide shelter. Some cows and sheep walked about, but even they looked cold and miserable. However, the inhabitants had important information to give, and the crew were told of warmer weather further south, and also of fierce brown warriors, called Skrælinger (Indians), many of whom lived in small towns with houses.

Even more intriguing was the story about Leiv Eriksson's younger brother, Torvald, and his expedition. Torvald's expedition had been up and down the Vineland coast for a long time. In the south they even had to take the ship up and tar it because the toredo worms played havoc with the unprotected hull. This gave them time to do other things as well. One of Torvald's men had stayed in Vineland, his name was Magnus.

"We made wine," Magnus said, "from small grapes we harvest there. You crush the grapes and time takes care of the rest. You get yeast, and from yeast and sugar you get alcohol." He laughed. "Not very good wine maybe, but at least it is alcohol."

Magnus also told of great fishing, how they easily caught all the fish they needed in the rivers. He told of an area where people lived in mounds made as huts (Georgia) and how they had a fight with the Indians, eight of whom were killed. Einar listened politely while he drank the mjoed, as Magnus explained how Torvald's thirty-one men had later been attacked by a superior force of avenging Indians and had to withdraw. 'Poor planning,' he said to himself, 'obviously the Indians are not much as a fighting force.' The words would later come back to haunt him.

"I have a wound under my arm," Magnus said, pulling up his sleeve showing a dark scar almost shaped like a bolt of lightning.

"Torvald had the same scar," he said," but he died from his wound. We buried him there and named the place Cross Ness. The year after we went back to take Torvald home, but Odin sent bad storms and diseases. We almost gave up. The expedition was led by Gudrik, Torvald's widow, she forced us to continue. We lost many men, but finally made it. Torvald is now buried in Brattalid."

Just like Einar, his crew did not place too much faith in the concern expressed by the Indian stories. Many of them had fought great battles against well-armed soldiers in Europe—what could some half naked wild men possibly do against Norse steel and swords? Surely previous expeditions had allowed themselves to be surprised and coerced. The crew was confident they would not make that mistake.

More important than the Indian stories however, they were told of endless forests, large rivers, and a land with abundant wildlife, much of it surprisingly easy to catch. Those who had been on these voyages gave them recommendations for their travel, including descriptions of fjords to avoid and places to be careful. Most intriguing of all were the stories of cities of fabulous wealth far to the south. Though mainly secondhand stories, they created big excitement with the crew, and all were eager to leave. As soon as the ship had been provisioned, they started south. The weather was warm, and the crew excited. It was easy sailing, and navigation even easier since they just had to keep the coast to their right, i.e. western side.

They continued south day after day, for weeks. The days grew warmer; the forest was green and endless. The trees were bigger than they were used to, one so big four adult men had to hold hands to circle it. The land was inviting in a beautiful way, yet also frightening in its enormity. One day they sailed through a wide inlet and up a wide river. Einar had never seen a river like this in Scandinavia, but he had heard of vast eastern rivers in the land where the Rus [*today's Russians*] lived and also in a far off place called Egypt. It was clear that what they traveled on now was a river. The water was first brackish, then fresh. Strangely it was not very fresh tasting, because it had a lot of sand in it, but by filtering it through some rags it was drinkable. The river was so wide it was easy to sail, and they kept far enough from shore that they would be able to spot any enemy before it became dangerous.

CHAPTER 3
The New Land

At a huge bend in the river, Einar decided they would go ashore to replenish their ship with fresh water and food. Almost the whole crew ventured out to gather berries and look for wild game. Espen and Einar were hunting together. Einar was never sure about Espen. He always seemed to be hiding his feelings, never letting his emotions show, always on guard. Nevertheless, their hunting foray was a success, and between them they managed to catch three squirrels and two rabbits, good nutritious food, and fresh. As they were skinning the game, it was as if the forest went quiet. They both sensed danger and dropped quietly to the ground. *Swoosh!* They could almost feel the wind as an arrow flew between them. Quickly they got their weapons out, ready for anything. The beautiful forest was quiet, but now it suddenly felt threatening. Einar motioned for Espen to circle out to the left, while he would circle over to the right. Quietly he crawled forward in an effort to get behind the assassin. The soft undergrowth hid his movements, but gave all sorts of insect's free access. After a few minutes he was where he thought the archer must have been. It was empty, but another sound could be heard close to him. With nerves on edge he was just about to charge when he realized it was probably Espen.

"Espen," he whispered quietly.

"Here," came the answer. "Did you see anybody?"

"No." They remained quiet for a while, but as the forest sounds seemed to come back to life, they realized the assassin had escaped, and both got up. It was quiet and nothing moved. Was the enemy still out there, hiding? They slowly retreated, on guard, then found the arrow lodged in a tree. It was Norse. With a jolt Einar comprehended what this meant. There was an assassin after all. Well, he knew it was not Espen, so at least he could take one 'suspect' off the list.

"Who would try to kill you?" Espen asked after he recognized it as a Norse arrow.

"Do you have any enemies on the ship?" Inwardly he was wondering if the arrow was meant to kill

Einar, or if it was a warning for him to do the job or face the same dangers himself. He assumed the latter. After all, who could miss on a shot like that?

Einar was thoughtful.

"I don't understand why they want to stir up trouble here," he said.

"Who are they?" came the reply.

"As you know, I fought with King Olav," Einar said. "He had many enemies, and some of them seem to bear a grudge still."

Back in the boat, the assassin cursed himself silently. He had been a bit nervous and waited too long before he let the arrow fly, so long that both men had sensed danger. And so he had missed on the first shot, what should have been a sure kill. Einar would be cautious and aware from now on. Espen had been there, unfortunately for the assassin since he had hoped to find Einar alone. Contrary to what Espen thought, they were both out to kill Einar, but neither knew of the other, or had any reason to kill anybody besides Einar.

Einar, did not openly ask who had gone out with a bow and arrow, but he asked some general questions to find out who had been hunting wild animals. Espen had agreed to keep quiet about the incident, so as not to stir up trouble and suspicion on the boat. Many of the men had been hunting, however, and it was obvious Einar would not find the assassin at this juncture. However, by finding out who had been hunting alone he narrowed the field to six: Odd, a quiet, yet confident man; Wolf a master bowman; Rolf, not a very good shot (so Einar half dismissed him); Geir who had also fought for King Olav and thus was unlikely to be the assassin; Torkjel and Alv Askman. He would try to keep an eye on four of these six men, but realized that he was unlikely to solve the mystery before the assassin tried again.

Everybody else was in a good mood as the boat was reloaded with fresh meat, berries and fresh water. However as they continued south, they started to realize just how long this coastline was, certainly longer than the European cost from Norway to the Mediterranean entry at Gibraltar. It had to be an enormous island. The trees were a different type from what they saw in Europe, but the biggest difference was in human activity, or rather the lack of it. In Europe, there were big cities and farms many places, and you could not sail for a day without seeing at least one town or farm. [*By modern standards Europe would also have looked thinly populated at this time*] It was different here. Even when they ventured inland they saw traces of humans, but never met any. The monotony and emptiness of the forests was getting on the nerves of some of the crew, but Einar reminded them this was what they had been told to expect, and besides, they avoided fighting this way.

"Let us be satisfied with the state of things. Fighting is only worth it when gold and fortune are to be won," he said. Privately he was also beginning to worry. Would they really find any riches here, or were Thor's statements during their conversation in Iceland true. This island yielded timber and grapes, but not gold or other riches.

One of the crew, Snorre, got sick after eating unfamiliar berries, or it could have been from something else that they were not aware of. His stomach got bloated, and his breathing was uneven. The whole crew watched with scared fascination, discussing what was happening to him. Some guessed his illness was caused by the berries he had eaten, but most leaned towards a poisonous insect or snake. This seemed the most likely source since his neck and throat were swelling and became bluish in color. Whatever it was, he died after three days of agony without any of them being able to do anything about the pain. The event took some of the excitement out of the rest of the crew. He had been a depressing and moody fellow, not one to miss, but it reminded them all that there were dangers in this new world, as in the old. Different dangers maybe, but dangers nonetheless.

After more weeks of slow sailing southward, the time came to set up winter camp, the way Vikings had set up winter camps many places in Europe, particularly in the British Isles. Ground had to be cleared, seed sown and game hunted. They sailed up another huge river to find an appropriate place. Einar hoped the Indians had not spotted them, but he was wrong. The Indians had known of their arrival from the moment they started up the river.

Chihopokolis (bluebird) was ten years old. He enjoyed considerable freedom, as did most Indian boys of the Lenni Lenape tribe, and his name came from his love for hunting birds down by the river. Last week's trip had been unsuccessful, but today would be different. He was going to show his friends that he was the real hunter among them. Ever since nine year-old Pukwes (Mouse) had speared two squirrels in one day, there was no end to his bragging. This boasting was doubly infuriating to Chihopokolis since Pukwes was a year younger. Besides, bird hunting to him was much more difficult than squirrel hunting, because birds take off from the smallest of sounds. After searching around the banks of the river, Chihopokolis found the perfect place and set up his little camp. The spot was both well protected and difficult to see. He covered himself with bushes and leaves and with incredible patience for a ten-year-old stayed completely quiet. But just as the birds returned and Chihopokolis thought he had perfect targets, they suddenly took off. Chihopokolis looked around to see what had scared them.

The sight that met him was unbelievable. He felt cold and hot flashes running through his body. All thought of bird hunting evaporated from his mind. A giant canoe under a white cloud was coming up the river. Chihopokolis stayed perfectly quiet, fearful that those on the vessel would see him. The creatures on this canoe where something else too, with hair on their faces and very strange clothes, some of which where shining in the sun. Chihopokolis pressed down towards the ground as the canoe came nearer and nearer. He wanted to run as fast as he could, but these might be gods, and they did not look like kind gods. He felt certain he could not outrun them. As the giant canoe passed twenty feet from him he could hear strange ugly voices. Surely these were evil gods! No Indian he had ever heard about would talk like this. He did not look straight at them. His father had told him that if you stare straight into a man's face, he may feel that you are looking at him. However, the sight was too fantastic to ignore and he had to look up every now and then, since this was so completely different from everything he had heard about in this world. Even the fairy tales the adults in his tribe told did not compare with this. Slowly the canoe passed him, only fifty feet away, then one hundred feet, before it rounded a bend in the river. Chihopokolis slipped slowly backwards into the forest, and raced home.

He stormed into the village shouting loudly, but since he was breathing hard at the same time nobody understood him. His father looked at him sternly.

"Calm down! Act like a brave, not a little baby!" he admonished. Chihopokolis pulled himself together. Still, it took a long time to describe what he had seen. Some of the adults were doubtful that what he'd seen was real, but the tribal leaders sent two hunters down to the river to take a look. Two days later they returned with frightening news. Chihopokolis had told the truth, and what was worse, the giant canoe had stopped a few miles further up the river. Not only that, the creatures on board were setting up a camp.

That night the tribe held a giant council. Opinions differed. Some felt they should stay away, others wanted to meet these strange people. The old medicine man fasted for two days, taking neither food nor water. He then smoked heavily from the magic big pipe. The preparation was successful and in his trance he ventured into the spirit world and talked to the gods. When he came back to this world, he was so exhausted even after eating and drinking, that it took hours before he could talk.

"These are dangerous men," he finally said. "The

gods told me we must be careful. Let us scout them out some more, then maybe meet them if things look good." The tribe agreed. Nobody dared dispute the words of the gods. They resolved that one hunter would always keep an eye on the strangers as a scout. The tribe could not decide what to do in the long run, but the decision was made for them. One day one of the scouts ran straight into one of the strangers, a female at that, in the forest. The white creature turned and ran before anything happened.

"Maybe they are not so dangerous after all," reported the scout. "They have women with them and seemed scared of just one brave."

The next day the tribal council decided to send men down to meet the strangers. Chihopokolis was allowed to go with the party. This made him incredibly proud, particularly since Pukwe had to stay. This would surely keep him quiet in the future!

As soon as landfall was made, Einar ordered the crew to start preparations for winter camp. A small palisade was erected for protection, more out of old habit than any real feeling of danger. No trace of Indians or dangerous animals could be seen, and the Northmen started to relax. It was not to last. Three weeks after landfall, Leone was out in the forest looking for berries when she felt somebody looking at her. She turned to see a young brown skinned boy gazing at her. More startled than frightened, she nevertheless turned and ran. It took her half an hour to get back to camp, and for every inch of the way she was half expecting Indians to jump out of the trees and kill her. The men grabbed their weapons when they saw her running and heard her shouts. They were ready for the worst. Hours went by slowly, nerves were on the edge, weapons at the ready, but nothing happened. They would have doubted Leone's sighting but for the stories they had heard in Greenland and Vineland.

When night came, Espen had first watch. It was one of the scariest nights of his life. The fear of the unknown was strong. At times he could swear he was surrounded by dragons and flesh eaters, but somehow they turned into trees and stumps when he swallowed his worst fears and carefully crawled towards them. He had plenty of time during the night to think about his mission to kill Einar. It was funny how the family fights and other feuds of Norway seemed distant here, unimportant in a way. Maybe he should just forget the whole thing for now since there would be plenty of time to carry out his deed when they returned to the homeland. But then he remembered the other assassin!

"Damn!" he swore to himself, indecisive about what he should do. After further contemplation, he nevertheless decided to wait before making any decision; maybe the problem would disappear by itself.

The next morning was beautiful, but nobody had time to enjoy it. An hour before the time when the sun reaches it zenith, a party of Indians came out of the forest. They carried food and weapons. The Norsemen decided to be friendly yet cautious. They stayed behind the palisades, swords and axes in their belts, but not in their hand. The Indians raised their hands, in a friendly gesture. Einar did the same. The villagers in Labrador had told them that the Indians, although they had different spoken languages, had a common sign language. The visitors consisted of males only, mostly men with a few boys thrown in. It was obvious they wanted some of the Northmen's weapons and knifes, but Einar's crew had agreed they could trade anything they had except their weapons. They gave the Indians some of their mjoed and the natives liked it and demanded more.

'They easily get drunk,' Einar thought. 'Maybe they are not used to alcohol.' The meeting continued, and although the mjoed induced drunkenness made the atmosphere tense, no incidents happened.

The next day women followed the male Indians, wanting fabrics and ornaments, offering furs in return. Einar's men looked at the Indian women curiously. In general they were shorter than the Nordic women, had wider cheek bones and darker skin, but many of the younger girls were very attractive, even more so after months at sea. The men tried their best to get to know them, with little success. The lack of a common spoken or sign language made the whole undertaking very difficult for men in dire need of carnal relief. Unfortunately the Indians had little to trade that would be of use to the Northmen, and after a couple of hours the atmosphere turned hostile. Some of the girls were obviously curious about these pale men, and likewise the Indian men were curious about these blond women, with a skin and hair color they had never seen before. In the afternoon Thorolf Scarface somewhat abruptly tried to get one of the girls to go with him to the tent, and in such a way that she started protesting in a loud and strange voice. One of the Indian men came over, and before anybody could intervene a fist fight broke out between him and Thorolf. Before Thorolf could get his weapons ready the Indian clubbed him with a stone axe, and a general fight broke out. Though brave, the Indians with their Stone Age weapons were no match for European swords and axes. The Indians retreated. However, Halvor and three Indians were dead.

"We have to leave," Einar said. His men wanted to stay, saying the Indians were no match for Northmen.

"They will be many more and they will be prepared for battle when they return," Einar responded, "and who knows, they may have better weapons with them. We were lucky, but there is nothing to win by further fighting, no riches in their camps. Let us find another place to stay over the winter."

As if to prove his point, a spear came flying out of the thick forest, lodging itself in Leone's thigh. They had noticed that none of the Indians used bows, but rather that a spear used with a spear thrower (atlatl) was the most common piercing weapon, an indication that the bow and arrow were unknown to these Indians.

The spear did it. They started packing up their gear in the boat. Leone was badly hurt so they decided to leave her to her own destiny. Some of the men felt they should just kill her, but Einar refused;

"We have to leave you here," he said, giving her some scraps of food. She was almost beyond herself with fear, begging him to take her along.

"You will die if we move you, but maybe these people can help you," he said without much conviction.

As so often before in her life, Leone could do

nothing. As her shipmates rowed away, one of the Indians came out of the forest and stood over her. They will kill me and rape me she thought, remembering things she had seen and heard in Europe, and for that matter experienced herself. But the Indian did not harm her, and later an old lady joined the man and put some leaves on her wound just as she passed out. Unknown to her, the Indians on the American east coast, unlike European warriors and soldiers, did not consider rape a manly thing to do.

When she woke up, Leone felt much better. 'It has all been a dream,' she thought, then with a shiver she realized she was inside a house, a stick house. The unfamiliar surroundings and smells caused fear to grip her again. She was naked under the blanket, but looking at her wound which had started to heal she realized she must have been out for several days. They must have undressed her while unconscious. The old woman and a man came in, took off the blanket and started to examine her. It was obvious nudity was not unusual to them, though the man was curious about her and touched her in intimate parts, rubbing her skin to see if the paleness would come off. He had never seen a woman like this, pale, tall and with full breasts. For a former trell such an examination was not that frightening by itself. Modesty was not something her social status had let her practice. Yet this was different. These people looked and spoke differently from anything she had known. When they left after a short while, she put the blanket back over herself, like a shield against a frightening world.

Later the old woman came back and fed her a nourishing soup of some kind, which Leone thought was not bad at all. After a few days with this care she was up and about. The old woman gave her a deerskin dress to put on. Leone smiled at the children and looked carefully about the camp. Her appearance did not cause too much excitement, so she realized they must all have looked at her while she was ill. Soon after she got up, the Indians started getting sick, and she was afraid they would blame evil spirits brought by her, something that would have been catastrophic. The disease had the symptoms of a cold, but was much worse. Two older warriors died. She comforted them as much as she could, not aware that it was her 'civilized' germs that caused the outbreak. North American Indians had very little immunity against European diseases, which a few centuries later would be one of the main reasons they were unable to stop the European onslaught. Leone could not know this. It was almost a thousand years before microbiology would give mankind any real understanding of the nature of diseases. Luckily for her, the Scandinavians were themselves partly shielded from diseases in their secluded homeland, and the flu she had brought passed fairly fast, without the Indians tying her presence to the illnesses.

As the days and weeks passed, Leone picked up more and more of the language. It was also obvious that many of the Indians were grateful for her help while they were sick. Even their village healer seemed grateful, but Leone sensed that in the future she had to be careful not to undermine his authority. The last thing she needed was an enemy here.

Despite her background, or because of it, Leone was good at reading people's feelings. Coupled with an intelligent active mind, she was able to immerse herself in the alien culture with remarkable speed and ease. She was introduced to new foods, noting that milk and dairy products were absent, as were cows. The meat was from wild animals, tasty and nourishing, mixed with a strange yellow plant (corn) which the Indians ate. The men were tattooed, some just in a minor way, but she did not know if that was by choice or had some meaning. In the evenings they would gather in the log houses and talk, telling stories that her limited understanding of the language would not yet allow her to follow. The women were initially wary of her, but when they realized she was no threat to them or their children, they started talking to her, helping her adjust to her new life. The children did initially follow her everywhere, almost to the point where it was a big nuisance, but after a couple of weeks the novelty wore off and she could explore the camp on her own. The man who had come to her sickbed smiled at her whenever they met, and seemed to like her. He was a rather handsome guy, not much taller than her, but with a muscular body and a nice smile. She liked that he did not have many tattoos. He was also clean, in a natural if not cosmetic way, compared to the Europeans. All in all the camp was clean compared to European settlements of the same era, mainly because nature could absorb pollution from the smaller Indian villages much faster than from the much larger European towns filled with domesticated animals.

She also noticed that the Indians looked very healthy now that the cold had passed. She felt more and more at home in the village, and liked her companion better and better. Her language improved daily, and she liked talking to him. Their background was very different, so it ended up that she told him about her hometown, and he told her the stories of his people. While she told stories about his people, she could read in her companion everything from attentiveness, to curiosity, to outright doubt. None of this was strange considering his surroundings. The ways of the forest, hunting and gathering seemed to be the only things he knew about, though he had some second hand stories about a city dwelling culture far to the southwest of them, called the Anasazi.

'At least we will not run out of conversation topics,' she thought. One of the rare traders coming through their village told of an elaborate city culture with hundreds, maybe thousands, of people living together. She was wondering if it was part of European culture, but decided probably not, based upon the description of the inhabitants and the fact that everything else around her seemed so different.

Leone's companion Suckeu Temakwe (Black Beaver) was an intelligent man despite his lack of worldliness. Finally he asked her to join him, in a ceremony which she realized was a wedding of sorts. She liked him, probably as close to love as she could come given her background, and she needed somebody to feed her. He was there and he was available. For him, it was much easier to make the decision to mate. He was at the tail end of the age when the men of his tribe married, and this woman was different and exciting. He sensed from the stories she told, that she had a difficult life behind her, and she had a certain aura of 'hardness' about her. Yet she was so desirable, what in a later age would be called sexy, that he could not wait to make her his wife. When he led her into the cabin after the ceremony they were both excited, and seeing his eagerness she had to smile. 'After all,' she thought, feeling an urge to giggle like a little girl, 'he treats me like a princess.'

And so Leone, who had for years been used and abused without much regard for her feelings, was treated well by what Europeans would later call barbarians. She smiled, but she did not laugh. A laugh could be misunderstood and she did not want to ruin the moment. Her past was history now, and as they joined together she thought she was better off than she had ever been before. She squeezed him hard as they melted together.

CHAPTER 4
The Maya

The ship sailed down the river, then turned south upon entering the ocean. Einar was brooding over the meeting with the Indians. It had not gone well. He remembered his own ideas regarding encounters with the Indians, and realized he had underestimated the difficulties they were facing. They had lost two more people, some of their wheat, and Olav was in a bad mood, having lost his trell. Espen said something to him and in return Olav lunged at him. In a second, a fistfight was under way. Einar struck out with the flat side of an ax, knocking Olav out, and leaving Espen in a daze.

"No fighting in the boat, you both know that!" Einar said when they came to. In a small boat no infighting while on board was the cardinal rule of behavior. He continued on a lighter note, addressing the women on board.

"We seem to be running out of trells to help the cook prepare the meals. You will have to take over their tasks and help Thorfast with the meals from now on." Up to that point, they had left the worst tasks to the trells.

They continued south for weeks. The open sea distances were much shorter than when they crossed the North Atlantic to Iceland and Greenland, and as the skillful navigators they were, it never entered their mind that they would not find their way back. Though far from home, their thirst for wealth and glory drove them on, the way lust for wealth has driven men on throughout the ages. It was easy enough to get food and fresh water, and nothing pulled them back toward Norway, not yet. They remembered and retold over and over again stories they had heard in Greenland about other journeys far south, and tales of vast cities and great riches. The water was getting warmer, and in some places they saw people in small villages and canoes, all of whom fled as soon as they saw the ship. The dragon head scared the Indians as much as it scared the villagers of Europe. However, despite the warmer climate, winter was still approaching, and the boat needed repairs.

They stopped at a small island to work on the boat. It was in dire need of major maintenance. An island seemed a safer bet now that they had the Indian encounter behind them.

"If we have to fight them again, let if be for gold or something worthwhile," Einar said. To be able to tar the bottom of the boat, he had a couple of the men build a skid they could pull it up on. This way, when it was almost out of the water, they could tip the ship over, first to one side and then to the other. After scraping the bottom clear of seaweed and shells, they replaced some of the planks, and then applied tar to protect the wood from toreo worms and other marine animals, all of which seemed much more active in the warm southern water than in the cold North Atlantic.

While some men were working on the boat others were on guard or hunting. There was a certain uneasiness about the whole place, not least because they were very uncertain about what animals could be eaten. To be safe they mainly ate fish, and as far as they could tell no natives lived on the island or in the vicinity on the mainland. The mainland was only a mile or so away. If somebody lived there, apparently they did not dare to encounter the Northmen. 'It is almost as if all the Indians have heard about us,' Einar thought.,' is that possible?' He was wondering if there was some kind of system whereby news traveled. It seemed unlikely but he was not certain. The girls from the boat enjoyed the luxury of land life, in particular the added privacy while having sex. On the boat everybody naturally knew what everybody else was doing at any given time. Gunhild found she missed Leone, though they had not spoken much, mainly a few words while they were preparing food. She felt sorry for her and, from personal experience, had a vivid understanding of how terrible Leone's fate had been. A trell among what must have been to her strange people. If she mentioned this to any of the other women they looked at her as if she was mad. Obviously they did not have the imagination to picture the fate of a mere trell, or to think that such a fate could befall them as well.

A few weeks were all it took before the ship was refitted. Being so far south, they decided to continue even though it was winter. In fact the winter here was as warm as a summer day in Norway. Gunhild looked at the island as it faded away behind them. 'Too bad,' she thought, 'the time on the island has been the best part of the whole trip.'

Initially they were heading almost directly south. However, they soon noticed that by following the coast they were turning west towards the sunset. Was this the end of the world?

"If it is the end, it is at least a beautiful end," one of the women said. Some of the crew wanted to return at this point, but the majority still wanted adventure and wealth. Steering straight west from the end of the peninsula, they crossed a large open stretch of water. It was now very warm, and it could be stiflingly hot at times, but the ocean breeze made it bearable. They were wondering how hot it would be in the summer. Compared to the overpowering heat and humidity on shore, they preferred to stay in the boat where one could easily cool off with water. They kept on going southwest, succumbing to the same drive that had earlier pushed other Northmen to

Greenland and Iceland, to the Mediterranean, through the endless rivers of Russia, and all the way to Constantinople.

After days of sailing they started to encounter islands. They decided to continue west rather than south until they reached the mainland again. This time they were greeted by dense tropical forest with strange animals and even stranger sounds, and they followed the coast southwards. But they never saw any riches, or vast cities. More malcontent surfaced, and as the days passed several crew members started talking openly of going north again. But their luck, if it could be called that, was about to change.

One day they anchored off a small island and during the night noticed fires in the distance, on what seemed to them to be the main island. Based upon their earlier experience, they decided to scout out the camp before encountering its inhabitants. Einar, Lars, Espen, Tor and Ole made up the scouting team. They constructed a small boat over the next few days and set off. Upon reaching the mainland, they hid the boat and started walking. The forest was dense, it was hard to breath in the stifling heat and high humidity, and there were insects everywhere, many of them biting and stinging. Einar prayed none of them were dangerous, causing the kind of sickness or death they had seen earlier.

After a two-hour walk they came upon what they had originally believed to be a village, and stopped dead in their tracks. Coming to their senses quickly they found a hiding place. Ahead of them was a sight unlike anything they had ever seen before. They had seen similarly sized cities in Europe, but that was where the similarity ended. The city in front of them was not like anything they could have imagined. In the center was a temple, a square, with steps leading up to a little house with a table in front of it. The pyramid was not smooth like the ones they had heard about in Egypt, but stepped, and there were torches on several layers and on the top. In front of the pyramid was a large plaza surrounded by what looked like homes of wealthy people, many covered with white stucco. To the left of the pyramid was something that looked like a market place, houses without walls but with a roof resting on stone columns. Some of the buildings were several stories tall, while others looked like large stone mansions and were lining smaller plazas. At the time of their arrival, the traders in the main market seemed to be closing up, removing the contents of their tables, which included various food stuffs, shells, beads and other colorful ornaments. Many of the vases and bowls were beautiful, both in color and shape. Despite their lack of wagons and horses, like one saw in Europe, it was obvious that many of the goods had to come from other regions. The different styles testified to that. The four men looked at each other, all realizing there were incredible riches in this city.

As they continued to look they also noticed murals and stone carvings. The images were of fantastic creatures, and some of war scenes. Very few, if any, had peaceful motives. The streets contained less garbage than commonly seen in European medieval cities. It was also noticeable that the buildings became poorer and smaller as you ventured away from the center. In the disappearing daylight they could see farms in the hillsides beyond, connected by trails and roads. Einar realized the city had to be two or three miles wide, and with several thousand people. They had been very lucky. The boundary they were on was the only side where the jungle stretched up to the inner city. From their vantage point it looked like the inhabitants had features common to the Indians they had seen before, so they concluded they were still in Vineland. However, contrary to the Indian villages they had seen glimpses of further north; there was something eerie and scary about this place. The drawings portrayed angry warlike gods, not beauty. Many of the people they could see looked like prisoners or slaves.

The main buildings were mostly made of stone, with the pyramid as the dominant building. Some of the inhabitants wore fantastic dresses, with incredible drawings and tattoos, but most were dressed lightly and some looked like they were slaves the way they followed what appeared to be masters or mistresses. The fact that so many people had ornaments made from what looked like gold, justified the Northmen's travel here. The problem was they could not really see how they could take it, considering all the people around. In addition, they assumed there had to be large numbers of soldiers, hidden somewhere.

Most of the people were facing the pyramid. As Einar and his companions watched in fascination, the top of the pyramid came alive. Two people who were later revealed to be prisoners were led up the stairs to the top of the pyramid. They were painted in a bluish color, and were bleeding profusely. They had obviously been tortured and were still struggling weakly, but as if in a trance. One of the prisoners was held by four warriors over the table. He screamed, or looked like he screamed, but nobody could hear him over the chanting and singing from the thousand voices. The continuous chanting was getting to Einar, he could feel his heart holding down the beat. He was sweating, not only from the heat but also because of the spectacle in front of him. A priest approached the prisoner held over the stone table, which Einar now realized was a sacrificial altar. The priest held a stone knife and quickly slit open the man's chest, taking out the still-beating heart, which he and the other priests proceeded to eat. The crowd went wild and their sweat could be smelled by Einar and his men. The man's body was thrown down the stone steps and other men proceeded to skin it. Now it was the other mans turn, his face showed such fear that Einar turned away, he had seen enough. The roar from the crowd told him the second man had met his end the same way as the first.

One of the guys tugged at Einar's sleeve.

"Let's get out of here before they see us! This is not something I want to experience up close." They pulled out and Einar felt exhausted. He had seen blood before, and other rituals, executions, and war, but nothing like this. He had an eerie feeling they could be the next lambs led to the slaughter. He told his men, except for Espen, to return to the ship. Espen and he would stay and reconnoiter the area. It was clear any open confrontation would be disastrous against such odds. However, there were obviously riches here, and the fact remained that nothing, at least nothing they had seen so far, could catch them once they were aboard the ship.

The problem was going to be how to get whatever they found or stole aboard the ship without being detected. As morning came, Einar and Espen were still hiding outside the village, trying to decide what to do. Two villagers came out and walked down towards the beach.

"Should we kill them and take their clothes?" Espen asked.

"No, we are too tall and fair-skinned to pass undetected," Einar responded. "If anything, we will have to take out two of the priests and steal their clothes, since their robes almost completely cover them."

The town was quiet since most villagers were still sleeping. One of the houses looked abandoned, and Einar and Espen decided to sneak in there. Outside, a giant statue of a strange human animal with giant teeth resided. It was almost too easy to enter the building, but once inside they found they were trapped. Daylight was coming rapidly. More and more people began to mill about, and there was no way they could get out before nightfall. Worse, they realized it was some kind of storage area, but for what they could not tell, since nothing was currently stored there.

The day passed slowly, and thirst began to bother them once they finished the little water they had brought with them. Looking out, they could see kids and adults playing some kind of ball game in a building close to the one in which they were hiding. In the early afternoon they saw people coming towards the storage house, and hurried to hide up in a semi-attic. If anybody climbed up they would be discovered immediately. Einar felt his heart pounding, and he had a feeling the Indians below would be able to hear the beat. Through the planks they could see that the priests had brought more prisoners to sacrifice, this time one boy and two girls. The young prisoners seemed dazed and scared at the same time. It was obvious from all the bruises they had that they had been beaten or dragged on the ground. One of the guards clubbed the boy in the head. He then grabbed the boy between the legs and squeezed. There was no motion, the boy was unconscious. He then proceeded to squeeze one of the girls. She wiggled in pain, and he laughed, saying something to the other man, who also laughed. Einar was ready to jump down. Despite all he had been exposed to, he disliked this kind of brutal, unnecessary bullying. In addition, frustration had been building up in him for days, and he longed for action. Espen sensed his anger and put his hand on Einar's shoulder, which helped his calmness return. It would be death to both of them if they were discovered.

The guard quickly tired of his game and left the young prisoners tied down on the floor. He exited the building. Einar and Espen looked at the girls. They were quite pretty. In fact one was beautiful, and Einar could not get his eyes off her. She was slightly taller than the other, and her face was not quite as wide. As the Northmen gazed trying to decide what to do, the girls started to come out of their daze. Blinking their eyes and shaking their heads, their eyes finally seemed to focus properly after a few minutes. They started surveying their surroundings. Suddenly they noticed the two men hiding above them. After the initial shock wore off, one of the girls said something to them. They did not understand her words, but then she held her tied hands out. It was easy to understand she wanted them to free her.

Tanama was coming out of her daze. What had happened to her?! She started to remember...

It all started some time ago, on a day that had begun early as most days did. As Tanama walked slowly down to the river to fetch water for her family, she watched as her small village of the Arawak tribe came to life. The huts were made of straw, around an open center. Some smaller animals scurried around. She could hear the smaller children waking up, demanding food and attention. There was something familiar and comforting about the morning sounds, and the morning was her favorite time of day. The air was crisp and clear, the stifling midday heat had not set in, and noises were still at a minimum. Soon shouting and yelling would start, but not quite yet, and she enjoyed the morning to the fullest. Her morning ritual was almost reflexive, since all members of the family had specific tasks to fulfill. This was the way it had always been, and nobody questioned it. Fetching water was one of her most important tasks. But as she leaned over the river bank with her jar, she realized something was different. The forest was unusually quiet. Most people living in close contact with nature develop a sixth sense with regard to danger, and Tanama was no exception. Puzzled because her people had long had peaceful relations with their normal enemies, the Carib, she nevertheless started to run back.

After only a few steps a war cry pierced the morning quietness. Gorily painted warriors, probably as many as 200, about the same number as the total number of people in her tribe, stormed into the village. She immediately realized they were not the Carib, whom she would have recognized right away. They had to be from the big Maya city far away that they had heard about. The few warriors of her tribe who were ready for action resisted fiercely, but were hopelessly outnumbered. She saw her father and two brothers struck down by stone-axes, and her mother impaled on a spear. Tanama turned to hide, but was clubbed to the ground by an unseen attacker.

When she came to, she was lying on the ground with the about seventy or so survivors, mostly women and young children, all naked. Blood streamed down her face and her hair felt sticky. One of the attackers grabbed her friend Sunflower by the hair and dragged her to the side. He forced her down on all fours, pulled her hair down hard under her armpit which had the effect of forcing her head towards her throat and chest and raped her there and then. As she got up crying, he clubbed her so hard her head split open. She dropped to the ground like a bag of fruit. The other warriors laughed. One of them grabbed Tanama by the hand and pulled her up. She was paralyzed with fear, knees buckling under her. In her terror she relieved herself. The sight of urine running down her legs made her captor laugh loudly, but it also saved her life. He let go, probably because he did not want to have sex with a blood-stained urinating woman. Tanama collapsed to the ground, relieved and still dizzy.

After they had gathered whatever valuables they wanted and forced the captives to carry them, the Mayan war band set out toward their home city. Hours and days of hard walking followed. Two of the young children were clubbed to death when, exhausted, they could not keep up the pace. Tanama could still not believe the tragedy that had entered her world. Her whole family had been erased in less than an hour. She walked as if in a trance, not noticing time or distance. After days of hard marching, they approached the big city where the captives, most of them crying quietly, too dazed and fearful to utter a single word, were split between the warriors.

The size of the city they entered made any thought of struggle or escape unthinkable.

"We will die here," Tanama whispered, halfway to herself and halfway to the prisoner ahead of her. There was no answer. The boy in front of her was too exhausted even to speak. As they approached one of the houses, their hands were tied up. A bowl was forced into her mouth, and she was forced to swallow a bitter tasting drink, which made her head spin. A little later her head started to clear up and she realized she was in a cabin, tied up, with a tremendous headache. The reality of her situation hit her hard, and tears began running down her cheeks. Only a few more hours to live, from now to midnight, then it would probably be all over in a bloody gory ritual. She had heard stories about that before. [*In fact they were not to be sacrificed, only men were, but this was not known to Tanama.*] She did not pray. What use would that be? Their gods had not lifted a finger when her tribe was exterminated. Obviously they had no power here, or were powerless against the mighty Mayan gods.

And then as the headache started to subside she noticed the two strange men above her. Fear gripped her again. They were fair-skinned with faces full of hair. She quickly came to her senses. They were men, not demons, and nothing could be worse than being sacrificed to cruel gods unknown to her people. She tried to talk to the men, but they apparently did not understand, so she held out her hands. They stayed where they were. She tried to reason with herself. They were not Mayan, and since they were hiding, they were probably enemies of the Mayas who could help her get back to her people. Then she remembered—there was nothing to go back to. Her eyes filled with tears as the hopelessness of her situation rolled over her. Suddenly the men above started to move. As they came down towards her, she thought maybe there was hope after all.

After a short whispered discussion, Einar and Espen decided to take the two girls with them. They could teach them Norse and learn what was around this area. If he was honest though, Einar knew acquiring guides was not the only reason for their decision. He just could not get his eyes off the tall girl. Her brown skin, beautiful hair, hips and breasts, were too much to bear after months at sea. She was dressed only in a loincloth that was more of a band which hid very little, and he felt desire swell up in him. He cursed at himself inwardly. Getting horny in the middle of an enemy camp was crazy. He reminded himself that there is a time and place for most things in life, and for now, desire had to wait. The two girls looked at the Northmen wide eyed as they loosened their ropes and made signs for them to be quiet. First the girls could not move, and then they gasped in pain as circulation came back to their hands and feet. Luckily they both had the wherewithal to keep their mouths shut. They all turned to the boy, but he was either dead or dying, so they left him on the floor.

They were silently waiting for the night to pass, for the sounds to quiet down, for the time when most people are sleeping deep. Just before midnight they heard somebody outside the entrance. Einar motioned for the girls to lay down on the floor and pretending to be still tied down. The guards they had seen earlier came in. They appeared drunk or drugged, and grabbed for the girls, expecting some fun, at least it should be fun for them. Their eyes opened wide when they realized the girls were free, one of them jumped up grabbing for his weapons. It was too late. Norse steel cut them both down quickly and quietly. After that they all waited, but nothing happened. Though their instinct was to leave as soon as possible, they forced themselves to wait until well past midnight, with every minute feeling like an hour. Finally the sounds from the outside started to quiet down. Einar motioned for all of them to follow him as he crawled out the opening in the back wall. They huddled down to be less conspicuous, but still their shadows against the walls, created by the torches, made scary shapes. Einar could not really tell if he was awake or dreaming, that was how surreal the whole situation seemed to him. He wanted most of all to run like mad, but forced himself to walk slowly, hoping that in the dark nobody would recognize them as aliens. Hunching down to hide their height the two Northmen led the way. They were going down one of the streets, staying as close as possible to the fence surrounding one of the mansions. Their shadows continued the wild dancing on the wall next to him. They were approaching the middle of the square. People were hurrying back and forth all around them. Einar became a bit disoriented. He thought he was heading in the correct direction, until he rounded one of many corners, finding himself face to face with a giant statue of a human animal with giant teeth. He knew he had seen that statue before. Suddenly he recognized it as the statue outside the building they had been hiding in.

"Damn, we have walked in a circle," Einar said. Espen nodded, the two Indian girls apparently guessed what he said, even if they did not understand the words. Cold sweat running down his back, he motioned for the others to turn around and go back. A man who walked uneasy came up to them, started to say something, realized they were strangers and opened his mouth to scream. With a punch born out of fear and desperation, Espen silenced him with one blow. He grabbed the man as he fell and carried him the way one supports a drunkard before dropping him to the ground around the corner. All four of them looked around with scared faces, but luck was with them. In the dark and among the thick throng of people, nobody had noticed the incident.

Now it was even harder than before not to start running, and Einar noticed one of the girls was white with fear, obviously close to panic. In fact Tanama did feel desperation running through her body, but just as she was about to scream and start running, she felt the hands of one of the strange men on her shoulder. She looked at him. He had a forced smile on his face and had one finger in front of his mouth, motioning for her to be quiet with a gesture known all over the world. The human touch made her overcome her fear, and she forced herself to continue the slow walk once again.

Einar was thinking quickly. This time he forced himself to be cool and level headed. They could not afford to go wrong again. He kept his bearing, and after a few minutes, to his enormous relief, he saw the jungle ahead of him, now they just had to find the trail they had used when they came.

"There," Espen pointed. Thank god, it was the trail; in the approaching daylight they both recognized it. As the group made their way through the forest toward the boat, they met a group of women returning from the ocean with fish. Einar hunched down to look unobtrusive. One step, two steps, they were passing the group of women rather closely, nobody acknowledging them in words or looks. He started to believe they would get away with it, but as the two groups were about to part in opposite directions, he saw one of the women go wide eyed as she realized these were strangers. She started screaming, joined seconds later by the others. Shouting from the city followed shortly. Their escape had been discovered. The only thing to do was to return to the ship as fast as possible. Fear gave them wings, and they practically flew down to the beach. With no time to retrieve their hidden boat, they jumped into one of the

Indian canoes and took off. They paddled frantically towards the ship, but knew the Indians with their superior rowing skills and familiarity with the canoes were overtaking them.

'Why didn't I destroy the other canoes?' Einar thought, cursing himself in the dark. Espen obviously had the same regret. Einar could hear him swear to every Norse god he knew.

Suddenly they saw the ship coming towards them, Ole at the steering oar. The Indians in their canoes hesitated when faced with the big strange ship, but then continued the pursuit. They all reached the ship at more or less the same time, and the girls were practically thrown aboard.

Espen, Einar and the other Northmen fought off the Indian canoes. One of the mightiest warriors, Wolf, even jumped into one of the canoes, emptying it with a swinging axe. It was a tremendous fight. There must have been a hundred Indians, but they were at a disadvantage trying to take a ship were men could stand steady and fight with better weapons. Einar found that his sword cut through the Indian shields and protective clothing like butter, while their stone clubs did minimal damage to their own shields and helmets. In the fierce fighting, men were screaming, cursing and dying. Einar realized he was screaming like a madman, screams born out of frustration and fear from the long hours in the Mayan village. At the same time he chased down Indian warriors with his sword. He controlled himself with a tremendous effort, and stopped the screaming. An unusually large Indian warrior came towards him, club raised. Einar barely had time to raise his shield, but did so just in time. Nevertheless his arm stung from the powerful impact of the Indian club on the shield. Now it was Einar's turn. His first blow cut the handle of the Indian club in two. The Indian realized he was defenseless and frantically tried to jump back in his canoe. He did not stand a chance, Einar's blow sent his head spinning into the air. That did it. The rest of the Mayans retreated amid the moans and screams of their dying and wounded men. The whole fight had only taken fifteen minutes, but it was a memorable fifteen minutes for all involved. The crew quickly killed the few wounded Indians in the boat or in the water, then the Norse sail went up and the Longship steered towards the open ocean. Nobody could catch them now, which was just as well, they were all exhausted after the short but intense fight.

Unbeknownst to the Northmen, they had created a legend among the Indians of big, fair-skinned, bearded men in mighty ships, disappearing under a white cloud. This story would later aid the conquistadors when they started their conquests, weakening the Indians' resolve in the face of the fulfillment of an old prophecy.

CHAPTER 5

The Retreat

The price of battle was terrible. Despite their advantage in weapon quality, seven of the crewmen and two of the women lay dead or dying, and for what? The fact that many more Indians had been killed was of little consolation. The bottom line was they had no gold, and they had a powerful tribe as an enemy with another retreat on their hands. To add to their woes, the ship had started to show considerable wear and tear, despite constant repairs. The fight with the Mayans had caused additional damage. The only good part of having a smaller crew was the lighter burden on the ship's food and water supply. They were down to twenty-two people now, including the two Indian women, and required less food. Unfortunately, the unexpected deaths also left them with fewer rowers in quiet weather.

Einar looked at the two girls. They looked frightened, but not terrified. After all, residing with these 'devils' was better than the cruel death that had awaited them before. The Indian females looked somewhat smaller than the Nordic women. He asked Gunhild to find them some blankets.

"This one is mine," Espen claimed, pointing to the shorter one with the wider face. Einar nodded in agreement. He had other problems.

The other members of the crew were obviously disappointed after they told them the story of the tribulations. They wanted to know if they should try to go back and raid for gold, but both Espen and Einar agreed that would be impossible. The Indian city was just way too large for a single ship to accomplish anything. They held out the thought that if they could get other ships to join them, it could surely bring plenty of riches for all involved. Despite the ferocity of the fight, all were aware that the Indian weapons were inferior to their own.

"So," Geir said, "what do we have to show for months of sailing, death and hardship? No fortune, not even anything resembling wealth."

"We will go north," Einar exclaimed. He found it best to stop any arguments before they started. "On the way, we will hunt for furs and other goods we can trade in Scandinavia. Hopefully we can establish trade with some of the tribes, and get additional riches that way. Next year we will be back with a fleet." The plan sounded empty even to him, and the crew looked unconvinced, but could offer no alternatives.

As if to add to his problems, Einar knew Gunhild and one of the other women were pregnant, and would probably give birth in a month or so. The crew would have to make camp for a short while when that happened.

The next few weeks were strange for Tanama. She and the other captive Macu, whose name meant Big Eyes, slowly started to learn the language. They were furnished with additional clothes to cover themselves. To have half naked women walking among the crew would be to invite trouble. Macu was used often by her savior Espen, and also by some of the other men, at first reluctantly but eventually with the sort of fatalism humans often show when faced with a situation beyond their control.

The strange thing to Tanama was that the dark haired man who had released her did not touch her, nor did he allow other men to touch her. She noticed that they were teasing him about it, and that he became somewhat embarrassed when they did. Tanama was both happy and uncertain about this; glad to be left alone, yet afraid a worse destiny awaited her! She could see in his eyes that he desired her, so why did he still leave her alone? The food, the clothes, even the smell of these seafarers were strange. Normally she would have been terrified, but after the terrible hours waiting to be sacrificed, nothing seemed so bad anymore.

Slowly she began to learn their language. After two days of seasickness, which had created much amusement among the crew, but not with her or Macu, she started to listen to and try to understand words and phrases.

"Einar," her captor said, and pointed to himself.

"Tanama," she responded, pointing to herself. At least she knew his name, though she found it hard to pronounce. He had kind eyes she noted, and was nice to her, giving her extra clothes as protection against the sea. There was another thing about him she found both strange and compelling. He had blue eyes. She had never seen that except on newborn babies, but found it very attractive. As everybody in her tribe knew, the eyes were a reflection of the soul and spirit, and with blue eyes it somehow seemed easier to read this spirit. As time went by she grew more and more attracted to him, forgetting his strange looks and hairy face, but always noting his eyes. With a shock, she finally realized she had fallen deeply in love with this strange-looking man with the beautiful eyes.

After the first few days, Tanama, and Macu, had to take part in the chores of the boat, mainly cooking. Privacy was necessarily rather limited on the small boat, but Tanama was used to that from her home village. At night she would curl up behind Einar, using him almost as a shield against the strange surroundings and an unknown future. At times she hoped he would turn around and kiss her or touch her, but he never did.

After four weeks they sailed up a large river and made landfall. They immediately started building palisades and a longhouse. The Indians left them alone, either because they had not seen them, or because they were afraid. The men and women worked fast and hard, keeping weapons within easy reach. In less than a week, a kind of fortified village was established, with three small huts. The weather was getting colder, but was still nice. Tanama and the other women gathered berries and firewood. She understood more and more of their strange language, but could still only utter single words, not phrases or sentences. On one of her berry collecting expeditions, Tanama ventured further than ever into the woods. It was beautiful here, cooler than where she had grown up, and the vegetation, though thick, was not nearly as dense as she was used to. Eventually she sat down on a fallen log, taking in the sunshine and the smells surrounding her. She was a picture of serene beauty, a young woman resting quietly under a majestic tree. She enjoyed the quietness of the forest, and needed this time by herself to come to grips with her faith. So much had happened recently. The loss of her family and of her whole way of life, the strange men that had rescued her, and the big ship that took her away from the only life she had known, all weighed heavily on her mind. Lost in thought, she started to doze off. Images of her past life—of people she had known, of scary Mayan warriors, of Einar's penetrating blue eyes—all blended together in a confused whirlwind that carried her away. There was her mother waving to her and she tried to wave back, but before she could move her mother disappeared on a beam of light. Her village came into view. She tried to reach out and hold it, but it too drifted away. Sunflower, the girl who was raped and killed, smiled at her but then her face shattered into a thousand pieces. Tanama felt like a speck of dust in mighty wind, carried back and forth, unable to control whether she was coming or going. She had no idea how long she had dozed under the mighty tree, when suddenly the noise of men fighting woke her from her uneasy sleep. Fearful, she got up and hid behind a tree.

Einar was one of the hunters. One of the benefits of being the chieftain was that he could usually choose the more enjoyable tasks. Today he wanted deer. Fresh meat was great after all the dried and salted food on the ship. After two hours walking, he came upon a beautiful stag, meat for days.

The forest was quiet as Einar carefully approached the deer. He was downwind and finally managed to get within fifty feet of his prey. The stag was tense, sensing danger, and ready to run. Einar flexed the bow, lowered it, and then flexed it again. Later he would never know what made him turn his head, but the move saved his life. The arrow that would have penetrated his neck just grazed him. Indians! Einar jumped up, grabbed his sword and ran towards the enemy, but it was no Indian. It was Wolf, one of the strongest crewmembers, one that Einar had barely talked to. Wolf raised his sword too as Einar charged towards him. With hate in his eyes after the sneak attack, Einar lunged. Wolf blocked, but Einar's sword had such power that Wolf could not stop it and it penetrated his side armor. Wolf's shock from Einar's quick reaction and the wound in his side both contributed to an uneven match. Einar chased him like a rabbit around the trees, before he finally delivered a fatal blow that almost severed Wolf's arm.

Wolf fell, bleeding profusely, trying to hold his arm together. Then he looked up at Einar, and realized he did not have long to live.

"Why?" Einar demanded. "Why?"

"You are an enemy of my family," Wolf revealed. "Many of my kin were killed at Stiklestad." The hate in his eyes was obvious, even though they had never had any personal disagreements. Einar looked at him, almost with pity.

"Since your side won at Stiklestad, why bother with me?" He asked. Wolf, getting noticeably weaker from the blood loss, opened his mouth to say something, but all that came out was a long 'Odiiin!' and then he fainted.

Einar lifted his sword, and in one strong swoop cut Wolf's head from his body, then left him there, wondering why Wolf had hated him so. 'Bastard!' he thought as he walked away. He decided to be cautious from now on. The tentacles of Norwegian family feuds obviously stretched far. There might be other assassins in the crew as well. And Wolf had been the perfect assassin, unnoticed, helpful, quiet, one you did not suspect before he stabbed you in the back.

Tanama was extremely happy to see Einar win. He was her only fixed point in a crazy spinning world. As he came towards her, she stepped out from the bushes.

"Tend wounds," she said in stuttering Norse. Einar, very surprised to see her, sat down. He wondered why she washed the wounds since the Northmen usually just bandaged them. As she did so her body touched his. It was almost like a spark flew between them. His arms slid around her waist, and he felt her arms close behind his back as well. He crushed her towards him, her mouth opened under his, and she took his hand and placed it on her body while she touched him. When it was all over, they were both lying in the grass exhausted. He had at times wondered why he had not taken her before. After all she was his prisoner. But now he knew he had wanted her to want it him too. Sex when forced was nothing like sex desired, and there was something about this dark-skinned girl, something in her eyes, her skin, and her desirable body that drove him crazy. And another thing was clear too, he did not want to share her. He knew he was falling in love, and it was not a good thing. The crew did not like their captain and navigator distracted by mere prisoners, however beautiful they were. They only wanted to get home. But right now he did not care. She was too close to him and he desired her too much. He rolled over and put his hand on one of her breasts, and within seconds they were making love again, slower this time, taking more time to enjoy each other, with the climax almost too much to bear.

When they returned to the camp, the others initially teased the two of them, but then noticed Einar's wounds. In a couple of sentences, he described what had happened, though he did not share his fear that Wolf was not the only crew member to have sided with his enemies.

The days went by slowly after this. The fall colors were strong in Scandinavia, but here it was almost as if the trees were painted. At least that's how it looked to Einar. They had seen autumn the year before, but now he really enjoyed the sight, marveling at the yellow and red leaves. Tanama kept asking Einar why this happened, but his only answer was that cold weather washed out the green color, not really convincing even himself. Her prodding made him wonder as well. It irritated him. A warrior should not be concerned which such useless knowledge. It was the way it was, that's all. However, the way she questioned many things he had always taken for granted made him question other things as well. One day they woke up to snow, wet heavy snow with a cold fog surrounding them. Winter had arrived, and though not as harsh as in Norway, it would eventually prove tough enough. The Indian women learned Norse rapidly now and could tell the rest of the crew about their strange and mysterious world. The Norse learned that the town they had seen was small compared to some of the other Mayan towns, and there were stories of other city dwelling peoples called the Aztec's and Inca's living even further South. According to legend some of them were living in huge cities with thousands of people. But the girls did not know if the stories were true or just folk tales.

'Like the stories of Odin, Thor and other Norse gods,' Einar thought to himself, too wise to say it out aloud. The crew was doubting him enough as it was. About half of them had turned to Christianity, but even they were still afraid of the old gods. It was better not to take any chances, you never knew, Thor's lightning strikes were known to all. One day around the campfire somebody wondered if it was the same sun they saw here as in Norway. This in turn led to a heated argument, and eventually led to some people not even talking to each other. It was a sign of how even the smallest things could grow out of proportion during the long dreary days of winter.

CHAPTER 6
Fire

With spring's arrival, everybody's mood improved. They had not yet seen natives here, although they had seen some traces of them. The men enjoyed the work on the boat, and the births of Gunhild's and another crew woman's babies were a joy to all. For all their toughness, the Scandinavians always cherished their own families. They were out of mjoed, but had a party nonetheless. Einar was happy, despite the poor result of the trip, and Tanama was the reason why. They snuck out of the camp all the time to make love, known to all but mentioned by few. He was almost sad when the ship continued its voyage north. They traveled slowly now since there were fewer rowers, and they were more dependent on the wind. The safety of the two babies meant they had to seek shelter if the weather turned nasty. In addition, they did not want any more skirmishes with the natives, and had to stop frequently to hunt.

Two weeks after departure from the winter camp, they entered another big inlet to hunt. While gliding silently through the forest, Geir, Espen and Eirik picked up the trail of a bear. Eager for variety from fish and deer, they started their pursuit. The forest was dense, with small ravines and boulders everywhere. Bear hunting was the king of sports, but bears were few and far between these days in Scandinavia, so they rarely had the opportunity. Bear hunting was certainly challenging, but it was also dangerous. Tense with anticipation and a little fearful, they saw the bear's trail go round a big rock. Should they follow? Eirik nodded, moving slowly around the rock, one step at a time. He sensed the presence of the bear, but could not see it. Then, out of the corner of his eye he saw the bear claw coming. He had looked the wrong way; the bear was behind the trees, not the rock. It was huge, bigger than any bear he had seen before, and red-brown in color. The claw lodged in Eirik's face, tearing out flesh and muscles. He immediately lost sight in one eye. Strangely enough he did not feel any pain. As if in slow motion, he saw Geir hurling his spear into the side of the bear, and Espen following with the shot of an arrow. The bear got furious, lifting Eirik up like a sack of potatoes, and hurling him into a tree. He could feel bones breaking and almost hear the blood rushing down his face, yet still felt no pain. Then he saw Geir thrusting his spear up under the chin of the bear, into the brain. It stuttered, falling down on its side. Espen and Geir came over covered in sweat and blood, looking down at him. Eirik tried to move, but his muscles did not obey any commands. 'That's odd' he thought, since he felt no pain. His companions looked down at him. It was a terrible sight, one eye torn out, the whole side of this face open so the bones were exposed, the angle of his body indicating that numerous bones had completely snapped. The one remaining eye was looking up at them for a few minutes, almost questioningly, but there was nothing they could do. The eye glazed over. Eirik had gone to Valhalla.

When Espen and Geir returned to the camp and told their story, the reaction of the others was mixed. Eirik had been a quiet, unassuming, but well-liked guy. At the same time, his demise meant more room in the boat, fewer mouths to feed, and bear meat. They all marveled at the size of the bear. None of them had ever seen one that large, except for the polar bear they had encountered at the start of their trip.

Despite their enjoyment over bear meat, the mood after Eirik's death was grim. The long weeks on the boat had taken a toll, and Eirik's demise was obviously another bad omen. They could almost feel something ominous drifting around, like a storm ready to break. The next day the explosion they were waiting for happened. Fuses were short, and in the evening two of the men started fighting over one of the women. Fortunately it was only a fistfight, but in the middle of it, one of the men was thrown into the fire. In the commotion nobody noticed the burning branch that flew up and landed on the boat.

What happened next was a disaster. The ship caught fire. Flames licked up the mast, and jumped over to the stores and onto the oars, all succumbing to the intense heat. After thirty minutes they managed to get the fire under control. They stood around the remnants of the ship, quiet, fearful of the future. Finally Einar opened his mouth.

"It can be rebuilt, but it will take us a long time," he announced. The plans came together, but as they worked on them they realized the new boat would be much smaller. They were short on tools and nails.

"We cannot cross the ocean," Espen said, voicing aloud what many of them knew but were reluctant to say.

"We don't have to. We only have to go to Vineland, there we can sign on as crew of another ship," was the answer.

"Some of us will have to go over land. We cannot all fit in the ship," somebody else said. The sentence seemed to hover in the air, motionless. Nobody was answering. Crossing over land, a land unknown, with mighty rivers and unknown tribes, a land filled with danger, it was not something anybody would do voluntarily. Quietly they split up, all deep in their own thoughts about the future.

The mood was somber and next morning Einar could see trouble was coming. Ottar, an expert axe man, but also a rather gloomy and menacing guy, came toward him followed by four other men, swords and axes in hand.

"You bring nothing but misery. Your incompetence knows no bounds," he said. "Your alliance with the new God and the Indian girl has made our gods angry. We will leave you here to die with your woman."

Einar knew the decision was out of his hands. He

had halfway expected the rebellion, knowing the distrust had been growing for weeks. He could have fought one or two, but not five. Ottar was a brutal man. Einar remembered how he had organized a game in England. They had let the kids of a captured village run away one by one, trying to hit them with a spear. The young children were easy to hit, but about half of the older children got away. Einar had participated, but deliberately missed. One of his men had refused, and was afterwards taunted with the nickname 'baby lover'. Ottar's last spear throw was a masterpiece. A little girl was trying to dodge the spears, but Ottar hit her at over a hundred yards, literally nailing her to the ground. The men roared with appreciation. The little girl tried to wiggle out, whimpering. Even to hardened warriors it was distressing, so one of the men went over and knocked her on the head with an axe, the little body going limp. Einar could not forget that sight, and could only imagine what cruelties Ottar would inflict on Tanama if he lost.

"I will go over land," Einar said, trying to forestall any unnecessary fighting by agreeing rather than putting up a fight. The five men half expected this. After all he had been the captain of this doomed voyage, and was responsible for some of their misery.

"I will go with Einar," Espen said, followed by Gisle.

"We will also!" It was Gunhild. Geir looked at her in astonishment, then nodded quietly. That made eight people off the ship, since the trell, Thorfast, and the two Indian girls would obviously stay. The rest would be able to fit into the new, smaller ship. Gunhild had volunteered because of her baby. She knew it would have next to no chance of survival on a small open ship hugging the coast. The baby had given her a purpose in life she had never had before, and thus for the first time she had made a decision. Her heart was pounding when she said it, but then triumphed when Geir nodded.

Once the decision had been made, work on the smaller boat continued apace. Einar and the others helped out, while also planning their own trek. Finally the day came when the ship departed. The twelve on the boat sailed off. But a small boat on the Atlantic does not have much of a chance. The boat perished, like so many before and after, their story unknown but to themselves.

CHAPTER 7
The Trek

The eight people left behind watched the little boat disappear in silence, each lost in his or her own thoughts. The three women were not too unhappy to see the boat disappear. The Indian women knew it left them in an environment that was at least partly familiar. Macu did not like to serve these men sexually, some of whom were anything but gentle, and the disappearance of the boat fortunately put an end to that. Gunhild was tired of the cramped conditions of the Longship, and had no special desire to return to Norway. It had been a life she did not particularly care for. Here at least she and Geir were together as man and wife, with no alcohol around. Despite his failures as a leader, Gunhild still trusted Einar more than she trusted Ottar and the other men. Geir was unhappy about the decision. He wanted to go back to his hometown, but these last few weeks he had also grown more attached to Gunhild, and didn't take her for granted the way he used to. His initial thought was to go, but he felt Gunhild would stay and realized he would rather be with her and Einar than risk his life with Ottar. Ottar was a strong man, but Geir did not have much faith in his abilities as a navigator and leader.

Espen had the most complicated feelings. He wanted to go back to Norway, but only as a rich man. Otherwise he would remain a servant to his father and older brothers. He now regretted his decision to share Macu with the other men. Initially he had done it to win their favor and gratitude, but after a while he had compulsions about his decision. By then it was too late. To stop them would have involved bloodshed, and he was afraid much of it would have been his own blood. Macu had 'grown' on him, not love maybe, but rather 'pride of possession.' Instead of leaving Macu, he decided to stay.

Thorfast also remained, but as a trell he had no choice. No free man would let a trell take his place in the boat, particularly since they had all seen the boat as their best hope for survival. Thorfast did not particularly care. His life was miserable in either case, but at least here he might escape. Maybe there was a land-bridge back to England that they did not know about!

Einar, like Thorfast, did not particularly care one way or another, but for different reasons. He knew their chances of survival whether in the boat or on land were slim. He could not have gone back to Norway without accomplishing his mission, even if he was no longer fugitive. After the story of this voyage was told, he would have been the laughing stock of the community. His family name a disgrace, with uncles and aunts living in shame. No Northman would freely let that happen. It was better to be lost or dead.

Their trek by land would follow the coast. It was agreed they would leave signs at the campsites they used on their way north. The intention was for the crew on the boat to send another Longship from Vineland to search for them. They did not have much hope. Einar was fairly certain the mutineers would not even bother to send a ship after them. At the same time he liked the fact that they traveled north. He longed to see the northern lights, the blanket of the gods, that strange phenomenon that reached down from Valhalla in the winter. He felt he would be able to pull it over himself like a protection against heat, humidity, insects, and all the things he disliked in this new hostile world. He felt an intense longing for the clear fresh air of the north, for the long bright summer days, and even for the biting cold. It was strange how things you disliked in the summer became desirable in the winter and vice versa. But the reality was that they were stranded in a strange land, and they had what felt like an endless trek ahead of them. If they were to have any chance to survive, he had to concentrate on the task at hand, not drift off to what could or should have been.

Navigating by the sun, they headed north a few miles inland from the coast. They followed trails made by the Indians. It was hazardous to use existing trails, but to make fresh trails through virgin forest would have been too strenuous. They met nobody the first few days, passing through beautiful forests filled with wild game, crossing small rivers, and passing lakes and ravines. The climate and environment were not unlike what they would find in Northern Europe, except warmer and with bigger trees.

Despite the beauty surrounding the group, gloomy thoughts descended upon them like smoke from a fire. They were so few, the forests were endless, and they knew that they were unlikely to survive any hostile encounter with Indian tribes. Nothing seemed to be the way it should be. The grass was not green enough, the sky had the wrong blue, the flowers all smelled wrong. The magnificence of the landscape was lost on them as they became more and more introverted. They grew more quiet, answering each other in single words instead of sentences, griping at each other whenever they had an opportunity, and quarreling over the best animal parts when they ate. Only their interdependence and the readily available food and game prevented total despair and actual fighting. This went on for days. Einar knew he should do something to raise everybody's spirit, but he just could not bring himself to do so. Even Tanama's closeness was for once not enough to break his depression.

A week after departure, on another warm day, it was Geir's turn to go hunting. As he glided quietly through the forest, he saw a small unfamiliar animal, with black fur, and almost like a cat. Getting his arrow ready he walked quietly towards it, staying downwind. He noticed a strange smell, but thought it came from a dead animal carcass or some strange plants. Then, just when he was finally close enough to prepare his bow, the strange animal suddenly turned and squirted straight at him.

"Odin, what a smell!" Geir cursed as he turned and ran, tears running from the stench and irritation to the skin. After a hundred yards he slowed down, but still the smell stayed with him. His eyes continued to water and breathing was uncomfortable. He realized the foul smelling animal was not pursuing him so at least it was not dangerous in the normal sense. He found a small stream where he tried, unsuccessfully, to wash off the smelly substance. When he came back to the others, they waved him away as soon as he was within smelling range. Even when he tried to describe what had happened, they kept telling him to stay away amid much laughter. He went back to the stream and made another effort to get the stench off, but it proved difficult to completely erase it. His eyes kept watering for hours. Eventually he discarded all his clothes and cut his hair as short as he could. Even then it took a couple of days before the others would let him close. It was a full week before Gunhild would let him near her at night, telling him the stench was a complete turn-off. But the skunk had broken the ice. For the first time since they started their trek, they were laughing. In fact they were laughing so hard they had to stop walking for a while. It took a couple of days before Geir could see the amusing side of what had happened, being the center of all their jokes and ridicule. Nevertheless even he realized how the cloud of despair that had been hanging over them lifted. True, they were still in a difficult spot, but they allowed themselves to be human again, laughing, talking, and loving.

Even the next incident took on an amusing overtone. Tanama had wiped her behind with leaves, but shortly after that her skin started to swell and irritate. It got stripes and welts, and for some time they were nervous that it was a disease. Apart from the itching she felt fine, so they started to relax. As soon as the fear of disease disappeared, the others starting joking with her, inviting her to sit down, slide down hills etc. Einar played along and put a good face on it, but he felt uncomfortable about the others making fun of Tanama's rear, and even more so when they looked at her skin. Having grown up in an area where nudity was pretty common, she made nothing out of showing them, but Einar decided Tanama's bum and private parts were definitely something he wanted nobody else to see. He told her so in private, and though not really understanding why, she did as he pleased and kept herself covered after that. After a few days the swelling was gone, and they all knew what poison ivy was by now.

The most amazing thing, Einar thought, was how the forest did not seem as threatening as it once had. It was as if the colors became friendly and bright. Now they could enjoy the moment and forget about tomorrow. When Macu mentioned a few days later that they all looked more and more like Indians, they were taken aback but soon realized she was right. Even that became almost like a joke. They had discarded most of the heavy equipment, including body armor and helmets. It was just too much to bring along since they did not have any animals to help carry them. In their new clothes one had to be fairly close before seeing that their features were not Indian, the main distinguishing mark being the men's beards. Einar would have given his left arm for a horse to carry the things they had left behind, but when he had tried to explain horses and mules to Tanama she just looked at him strangely. The animals she could describe where nothing like them. In a strange way, the skunk had become the pivotal moment of their trek, the moment when life seemed to have meaning again after all.

The momentous event that had been in the back of all their minds came three days later. They stumbled upon a village, so well hidden they did not see it before they practically bumped into the first hut. Strangely enough, the inhabitants had not seen them coming, and both sides looked at each other in astonishment. Einar felt his hand gripping the sword, and saw his companions reaching for their axes. Before anything happened, Tanama and Macu stepped forward, hands held out with open palms, indicating they were traders. After a few tense moments, one of the Indians returned the greeting, and they all cautiously approached each other. The words spoken were not understandable to the Northmen or the two Indian women, but signs continued. Einar started to understand that the sign language was pretty universal among all the tribes, and obviously a necessity in a large country with a small population spread far in small tribes and groups.

They were led into the camp by the Indians, more relaxed but still ready for anything. The camp probably housed around a hundred people, children included, and there was something strange there. When they were sitting down around the centre of the camp, where wood had been stacked for a fire, the chief gave them a burning stick of some kind, from which he pulled smoke. Einar tried to do the same, but coughed and passed it on. The Indians laughed heartily and that broke the ice. The others had the same experience, coughing and passing it on. After this ceremony they could walk about the camp.

This was the first time Einar had time to see an Indian camp up close, and now with Tanama at his side, he could get a better understanding of some of the tools and weapons. At first he looked at their weapons, as was his nature. They had noted before that most Indians used spears, lances and clubs, but did not notice any bows or arrows. They could be divided into a few general categories. Their hand held weapons were mainly clubs and a primitive axe (tomahawk). Both had handles made out of wood. The clubs were both rounded wood, and in some cases with a stone fastened to the end. The tomahawk had sharpened stones, and in some cases copper ends. All were far inferior to swords and metal edged axes. The Indian offensive weapons consisted of the atlatl they had come to know, and a lance, which was basically a thicker spear. To protect their bodies some of the braves had a shield of heavy hide or bark stretched over wood. In addition some of them had body armor in the shape of wooden slats or rods tightly bound together. Einar noted some weapons that looked purely ceremonial, or at least the Northmen could see little practical use for them.

Everything considered, the Indians' weapons and protection were primitive compared to the European weapons, but would be deadly enough when used correctly. They were equipped as farmers, not warriors. Einar thought his group would be the better armed if it came to a fight even though they would most likely be heavily outnumbered. He reminded his men to keep their weapons close at hand at all times, and in good order. They were starting to show wear and tear after months of travel, though the animal grease they smeared on them had kept the rust at bay even if it had not completely eliminated it.

The camp, like most of the others they would see later, was laid out with small huts surrounded by small fields where corn was grown. Some tents and teepees were scattered among the huts. He noticed the Indians to a large extent lived off farming combined with hunting. In fact when the first European settlers came they took over abandoned Indian farms (left empty by disease) more often than they cleared their own land. The huts were constructed with vertical sticks, filled in with bark and grass, not the horizontal log houses so common in Northern Europe. They looked feeble, but as Einar thought about it, it made sense. Their Stone Age tools made logs much harder to cut, and there was no need to build terribly sturdy structures since they did not have to cope with the long Nordic winters.

Throughout their walkabout, Einar told Tanama he felt something was strange, missing from the camp. She, however, felt everything was in order.

"Look, "she said, "they are all here, the old, the young, houses, fields, what more do you expect?" Einar didn't answer, but he still felt something was strange. The camp was 'cleaner' than what he was used to from Europe, despite its many strange noises and smells.

Espen came over to them,

"There are no animals here," he said. Einar realized what the strange feeling came from. No pigs, cows or horses walked about, and consequently there were no smells from the dung, and no flies that came with them. The only animal kept was a breed of dog, if that was what it was. That's why the camp was 'cleaner!' The human 'leftovers' were easily absorbed by the surrounding nature, without all the animal waste added to the human waste.

He also noted that the Indians looked remarkably healthy. Was it their diet? Einar did not know it, but he was pretty close to the truth. Before the white man's diseases came, the Indians were very healthy, shielded by the ocean from the contagious diseases of the rest of the world. Not keeping domesticated animals for food production to any great extent, they also avoided many diseases coming from such animals, like anthrax. In addition, meat from wild game has much less fat on it. Unfortunately this healthy lifestyle also meant that they had not developed much immunity to the diseases of the old world, something that would be one of the main factors in their losing contest with the whites 500 years later.

"Tanama," Einar asked, "why are they so friendly, compared to the other Indians we have met?"

"You look almost like Indians now," she said, "and there are very few of us. We are not a threat." With a shock he realized she was telling the truth. They did not carry much with them, and their European clothes were mostly gone, having been replaced by leather clothes made during their trip. True, their beards which they cut as often as possible, swords and axes were different from Indian equipment, and their skin was lighter, but that was pretty much where it ended. He looked at her. She looked more beautiful than ever having recovered from the sea voyage. "Come," he said, leading her into the forest.

They found an undisturbed spot under a big tree and made love passionately. It just gets better and better, he thought as he looked at her naked body resting next to him. Her hips, her delicate breasts, the inviting triangle between her legs, her full lips and slightly wide face were almost too much to bear. He was actually happy, despite having lost most of his possessions and having little hope of returning to his home.

The next few days were peaceful, but they still felt an urge to continue North. They bid the tribe farewell, a small group traveling through an enormous land and endless forest. Weeks went by. They continued ever northward, having only friendly encounters with the natives. Their group was too small to be a threat, and their appearance created curiosity rather than fear.

One thing they noted was how different the Indians' camps were from each other. They differed in size from a couple of huts to camps that covered several acres. Housing was also varied, from straw cabins to teepees, the latter used by nomadic groups. The cabins were not universal either, though the building styles seemed related between the tribes. For the farming communities, plants, mostly corn, seemed to make up more than half the food supply, with the rest covered by hunting and fishing, and collecting berries and edible plants. The language and customs also changed the further north they came, but most of the tribes they met seemed to belong to the same group. Their dialects, dress and customs varied, but there was a commonality between them.

Their progress was painstakingly slow, just a few miles per day, slowed down even more by the need to hunt and gather berries and other edible plants. Eight weeks after their departure from the tribe they ran into trouble again. It started innocently enough. They were staying close to a friendly Indian camp. One morning Macu went into the forest but came running back yelling

"Attack! Attack!" First they thought their new friends were going to attack them, but she quickly explained that she had seen a more powerful tribe preparing to attack their friendly neighbors.

The Northmen quickly went into action. Einar threw an axe to Thorfast.

"Let us follow behind them as they approach. They may not be aware of our presence," he said. They did as he said, and the moment the tribe attacked their neighbors they charged their common enemy from behind. The attackers were taken completely by surprise. The European weapons cut through their stone-age weapons with ease. Einar's sword cut one of the men's torso almost in two, Thorfast's axe crushed a man's shoulder. The attackers ran away, but the Northmen cut down the stragglers and the wounded.

The tribe they had protected looked at them with gratitude but also with fear. Indian warfare in general was not this bloody. A few died, but most raids were for prisoners and possessions, and later for horses. European warfare, which involved annihilating your enemy, was relatively uncommon among the North American tribes.

After they had buried the dead, the Indians held a ceremony to celebrate the souls of the dead enemy, as well as thank the Great Spirit for the victory. The tribe had lost only one young boy in the attack. After the ceremony, the old chief came over to the Northmen. Through sign language, and the few words they could exchange, he told the Northmen he wanted them to leave.

"The Great Spirit has given us a great victory, but with so many dead our neighbors will thirst for revenge, and we fear the future."

As they got ready to leave, Thorfast refused to give up his axe.

"I am a trell in Norway, but free here."

"Let it be so," Einar said,"You are one of us now." They were a small band in a big land, and needed every man they had. They could make Thorfast a trell again if they ever returned to Norway.

The attacking tribe they had defeated lived to the North, the very territory they had to travel through.

This slowed down their progress, and they were extra cautious the next few days, avoiding any contact with the natives. They kept going north, and were optimistic about avoiding fights. The day marches were shorter than before because both Macu and Tanama discovered they were pregnant. This was disturbing to Espen, since he had no idea if he was the father or not. The news ate at him, leaving him in a grim mood, and less observant than he should have been.

The attack came out of nowhere. Espen did not even hear the Indian spear thrown from the atlatl as it passed close to him before it hit Geir in the neck. For a split second Espen looked in shock at the ends of the spear sticking out on opposite sides of Geir's neck. Then he reacted, charging towards the attackers. There must have been about twenty of them, and they did not expect the Northmen to counterattack. A few of the aggressors threw their spears away as they fled, wondering what kind of devils they had encountered. Espen followed them like a madman for a few wild minutes before he came to his senses and stopped.

'I am not going berserk,' he thought, 'I have to get back to the others before I get lost.' When he returned, his companions were all looking at Geir on the ground, the spear rotating grotesquely every time he drew a breath. Nothing could save him and they did not even dare to extract the spear.

Geir looked up at the sky in astonishment. Why was he on the ground? He did not feel any pain. He had not seen anything, only felt himself being thrown to the ground. He saw Gunhild looking at him with fear and tears in her eyes. 'Why? She is beautiful,' he thought, realizing he had probably not been as good a husband as he should have been.

"Take care of my son," he said to her, but the sound was only in his head, nothing passed through his damaged neck. It was getting dark he noticed, kind of early for that. How peaceful and nice the forest was. He had never really noticed that before, and how could it be that his mother was approaching him?

They buried Geir quickly, fearful of another attack. All were grateful to Espen for his quick and decisive action. Though they did not know it, the Indians had decided to leave them alone. The small bands of Indian tribes never wanted to fight if they could expect a large death toll. This was not for lack of courage, but rather for the preservation of the tribe.

Gunhild walked on as if in a daze. She had never loved Geir deeply, but he had been a good man, and what would become of their son now that he was without a father? When they got back to Norway, who would want to marry a poor widow with no land and a baby to take care of? 'It's not fair,' she thought, 'not fair! Why didn't the spear hit one of the others, Thorfast for example, or one of the Indian girls? Anybody but Geir! It's just not fair...'

Macu had been wounded by a war club thrown by one of the attackers, but she could still walk. Tanama carried some of her things. Macu looked over at her gratefully. She had not really known her before they where thrown into the Mayan hut, but now Tanama was her anchor in a hostile world. Tanama had blossomed and filled out. She was more beautiful than ever, and Macu knew why. Tanama was in love, and was being loved in return. Macu wished that

Einar had chosen her instead. If he had, the sea voyage would not have been such a nightmare for her. Life was better now that she only had Espen to take care of, and it was obvious he cared more and more for her. Nevertheless, she could not forgive him for what she had been through with all those foul smelling brutal men on the boat. His negligence took away from her what should have been given after a ceremony in the tribe, marrying her to one man. She could never forget, and never forgive, but for now she accepted her destiny out of necessity.

On the trail later that day Espen approached Einar. After much consideration he had decided to level with Einar.

"We need to talk," he said. They walked a little ahead of the others, and Espen continued "My family is related to Tore Hund's family, and another of your Norwegian enemies. I was sent to kill you."

Einar looked at him in surprise.

"There will be peace between us here," Espen continued. "You are a good leader. We have been unfortunate, but this is not all your fault. Sometimes the gods are against a man and there is little one can do. The blood feuds of Norway are meaningless here. If we ever return to Norway we will become enemies again, but not before that."

"Good," Einar said. "Let it be this way, "we will probably not return to Norway considering the circumstances we are in, and our blood feud is worth nothing here in this land. Survival is everything."

The difficult march over the next few days took a heavy toll upon them all. There was minimum time for hunting, or for caring for a baby and two pregnant women, and they were not much of a fighting force in case of another attack. They were a slow moving procession. To make matters worse, Macu's wound did not heal properly and she became sicker and sicker, her pregnancy complicating matters. Had the attackers used poison? They did not think so. Her wound looked like the infections so commonly found following battles. But three days after her attack, Macu miscarried. Though they knew the best way to make good time would be to leave her, Einar and the others could not bring themselves to do so. They were so few, and the land was so big. After weeks together they had developed a certain relationship between themselves, and while it may have been partnership more than friendship, there was a mutual dependency borne out of necessity and familiarity. The small group continued slowly north, more aware than ever that any determined Indian attack would certainly wipe them out. They were all going hungry. It was as if the forest was empty of animals, maybe due to the almost continuous crying of Gunhild's baby. The baby's sounds were quickly swallowed by the forest so humans would have to be fairly close to hear them, but the ever alert animals were scared away. It was a vicious cycle: the crying scared away the game, less food meant they were less able to hunt and eat well, and hunger meant more crying. The wailing baby was getting on everybody's nerves.

Macu was getting better, but still had to move slowly. She did not seem to heal the right way, or with the speed they expected. Unbeknownst to the others it was more than physical wounds that hurt Macu. She could not reconcile her past ordeals. The scars were too deep, and seemed to grow deeper. In addition she was now growing jealous of Tanama. Even in the group's most trying moments Tanama somehow glowed, and Macu resented it, more than she could even admit to herself.

CHAPTER 8

The Old Camp

The mood among the little band of wanderers was somber. Not much was being said, and even less heard. Each in the group was feeling lost and lonely. As the summer heat started to abate, they reached a great river. Without the energy to build a float or a boat, they followed the Southern shore, even though it carried them in a northwestern direction. A realization dawned on Thorfast.

"This is the river on whose shores we planned to stay our first winter here,' he explained, "the place of the first Indian attack." A sense of renewed hopelessness settled on the group. Two days later they came upon their old camp, but in the midst of their despair came a glimmer of hope. The wheat they had sown on their first visit was growing wild now.

They gathered as much as they could, and crushed it to mix with water for porridge. With food in their bellies, the mood once again changed, and optimism returned. Tanama claimed she had never tasted anything as good. They all laughed, even Macu and Gunhild who were in worse shape than the rest of them.

"I will stay here," Espen said, "this is as good a place as any to die."

Einar's first urge was to remind him who was the leader, but when he gave it further thought, he realized they could not waste any energy on infighting. He may be the leader, but in this group of individuals he was not the captain. It had been several days before they were discovered last time, and now they were a much smaller, quieter and wary group. The decision about what to do could wait. The next day, they set about repairing the fence. At least they would have some protection, and from the safety of the fence even the women could fight well.

Their luck ran out a week later. Gathering berries, Gunhild looked up, straight into the faces of three Indians. They did not have war paint, she noticed, holding out her hand in the sign of friendship. Her heart thumping, she forced herself to stand still. The weeks and months with Tanama and Macu had taught her how to behave. Without a word the Indians turned and disappeared into the forest. She forced herself to walk steadily back toward the camp until she was under a mile away, then she ran as fast as she could, alerting the others.

The next few days were tense. They did not dare go outside the stockades, but no foe came. Then one day at least fifty Indians appeared, slowly approaching their compound.

"Nobody touch their weapons," Einar commanded, knowing that any fight against such odds would be brief and hopeless. He also noted that there were women among the Indians, and that was a good sign. There was something strange about one of the Indian women as well. She seemed lighter skinned than the others. Ten feet from their entrance, the Indians stopped and two of them stepped forward, one of them the light-skinned woman.

"We come in peace," the woman said. 'Good,' Einar thought, then froze. The words had been spoken in Norse. Suddenly he recognized the woman as Leone, the trell they had left behind to die. He was bewildered. She had obviously survived, but how. She seemed different also, beautiful in fact. He had never noticed that before. The Indians must obviously have treated her well. He had a thousand questions, but all he could utter in his relief was;

"We desire peace as well."

Leone told them to follow her back to the camp. Thorfast refused, insisting on staying put.

"Don't be a fool," Espen said. "They can kill us if they want to, wherever we are." The women agreed, and Thorfast gave in. The walk to the camp was tense.

Espen felt as if his feet moved in clay, and expected to get a spear in his back any moment.

The camp was bigger than most of the forest camps they had seen. As they marched through the village, villagers emerged from cabins, from around corners, and in from the fields. To the Northmen it seemed that even the dogs were curious. It was a friendly if skeptical stare, though, and they still felt uneasy. The events of their last visit were still fresh in their minds. Einar and the other men were asked to sit down by the big fireplace in the center of the village, the women seated right behind them. A pipe was lit and passed around. The adult men were quiet, but they heard the women and children talking in the background. Espen, Einar and Thorfast were dying to ask questions, but had learned how to behave. 'Have patience, always wait for your turn,' Tanama had advised them. What appeared to be the old chief of the tribe sat meditating with his eyes closed. Slightly behind him, an old woman was seated. She had more wrinkles than Einar would have thought possible on a human face. He could not even start to guess her age, though she looked older than the chief. Finally the old chief of the tribe spoke, with Leone as an interpreter.

"I am Newo Ahas (Four Crows), chief of the Lenni Lenape. My mother here is Wisaweu Mbi (White water)." Considering the age of the chief, the old woman must be ancient, Einar thought to himself, taking care not to stare or do anything that might be misconstrued as hostile or disrespectful.

"You came here many moons ago in big ship. A few of you are now returning. Woman of Black Beaver (he indicated Leone) told us that you did not come here to fight, only to trade for yellow metal further south. You do not appear to have been successful." Espen thought he saw a faint smile in the old chief's face, but he was not sure. A long pause followed, then Four Crows continued.

"We could have killed you, but woman of Black Beaver has told us we can learn things from you, and since you are big warriors, many of our young men would die if we attacked." Four Crows stopped for another long pause. Einar was just about to say something when the chief continued.

"We want you to stay here as our guests, and teach us how to build boats, use weapons that throw spears, and make hard points that shine."

It was now Einar's turn to respond.

"We are honored to stay here and live with your people," he said. "We will teach you the ways of the people across the great lake, and hope that our stay here will benefit both of our peoples." He decided it was better not to say too much right away, and he bowed and sat down.

After a while the chieftain and his men stood up, and this seemed to be the signal for the meeting to break up. The travelers all started asking Leone what had happened, and she told them her story.

"Now I have a daughter," she said, "and I am expecting a second child. My new name is Wisaweu Ochkweu (Yellow Woman), due to my fair skin and hair. I am happy here. These are good people. They treat me better than you did. We may look poor, but are not really so, for who is poor if there are no rich people around?" Einar looked at her with new respect. All she had said was true.

"Why did you save us?" he asked.

"I would gain nothing by having you killed. Revenge may be important for some, but not for me. As the old chief said, many men would die for no reason if we were to fight. I am happy, and you were never really cruel Einar, unlike some of the men," she smiled,"besides you did not tell on me that time in Iceland when I spoke out of turn."

Einar told her the story of their trip, and all that had happened.

"You should learn the language here," Leone told them. Over the next few days she taught them new words, helping with pronunciations. Learning was slow at first, giving the village children and adults much to laugh about. However, a few words were similar to what they had learned in other villages. [*The Delaware's were part of the Algonquian language family which covered most of the Northeast, including Illinois, Michigan, Wisconsin and Southeastern Canada. Within this general area, the Iroquois language group occupied what in a rather general term is Pennsylvania and New York. Algonquian subgroups included well known tribes like the Mohegan, Pequot, Powhatan, Shawnee and Miami. The eastern branch is not well documented since several tribes became extinct early on in the white conquest.*]

As time passed, the Scandinavians became more and more involved with life in the camp, eventually abandoning their original camp and setting up houses or tents in the Indian village. The men hunted, the women prepared food and kept the cabin orderly. Tanama was very happy, and she was pregnant. This was her life, and she connected very well with Leone, despite their different backgrounds. They had one thing in common. To a certain extent they were both strangers here. Gunhild and Macu joined them often, though Tanama never got as close to them as Leone. Gunhild had taken up with Thorfast, mostly of necessity, but strangely enough she found she liked him, and he her. The new relationship was easy to get used to for Thorfast, who needed a woman and was starved for sex after years as a prisoner. He was kind to Gunhild's baby, and after a short while she became pregnant again, despite efforts to avoid it. All in all they were both satisfied, but always keenly aware that they were among strangers. In a way this made them even closer as a couple. Macu was the only one who was not really happy. She missed her old tribe, and the mental scars and memories from the attack and the later ordeal on the boat did not go away. Indeed, they grew stronger and more nightmarish as time passed by.

For the group as a whole, the time in the camp was good. They adjusted to the routine and learned the language rapidly. The men still talked about how to get back to Greenland by boat or by land. Either way it would be a formidable journey. Their relationships with the men of the tribe were very good, so good that the Northmen almost felt at home sitting around the campfire at night. They enjoyed the family life in the cabins they had built with the help of their neighbors. They discovered many things, including the messages hidden in wampuns. These were not written words, but the symbolism could tell remarkably long and detailed stories. Trade with other tribes was limited, due to the lack of available transportation, but the wampuns formed a measuring system, similar to money in the modern use of the word. Einar thought one of the reasons for the relative backwardness of the Indians compared to the Europeans were the absence of horses. Without a large beast of burden, trade was naturally curtailed, since everything had to be carried or pulled by men or dogs. This meant relatively isolated tribes and slow exchanges of ideas. As a group, the Indians seemed of similar size to the Europeans he had encountered while raiding the continent. They were generally tall, straight and well built, walking with their heads held high, not in the subdued fashion he had often seen in Europe, where people seemed to look straight into the ground. They readily shared all their belongings, and nothing seemed too good for a friend. He noticed that a few Indians had beards, but most did not, and hair grew sparsely on their faces. In their hair, such as it was since most of the men had clean shaved almost their entire scalp, several Indians had long feathers. Leone told them the style the feather was worn in indicated which clan they belonged to. Einar certainly liked their less materialistic ways, it made for less warfare. The clothing was simple, the men mostly using a breechcloth with a belt, at least in the summer, while the women wore a knee length skirt, mostly made of deer skin. It looked quite attractive.

"You have to get one of those," he said to Tanama, "I don't like the men to see too much of you".

"I do," she retorted, "their interest keeps you from taking me for granted." The smile on her face was a little wicked. He pushed her away with a laugh.

"Maybe I should trade you," he said, "I would

probably get several beautiful animal skins for you."
They walked on.

"You have to give me some ornaments to show your love," she said, pointing to the ornaments several women wore around the neck. They were made from antlers and shells.

"I would dress you in gold and silver if I could," was the answer, but he did not see any gold or silver in this area, the way he had in the Maya town. By material standards, the dresses were extremely plain. He realized he had to find a way to obtain some jewelry for Tanama.

Half a mile from the camp was a stream. The tribe always built camp along streams, and the ready availability of refreshing water was a big consolation for all their other troubles. Every morning, except for the coldest days, Einar started the day with a short swim. Tanama started joining him in this, eventually enjoying it. They did it not so much for washing as for feeling awake and fresh. Most of their fellow tribesmen and Northmen, including Gunhild and Thorfast, thought they were crazy. Some of the village kids would even sneak down to watch them. Einar was just about the only person who could swim, and though he offered to teach them how, only a couple of the kids accepted. For the rest, water was something you drank or fished in, period.

The Lenni Lenape, or Delaware as they would later be called, were not nomads, but the tribe typically had a couple of villages they moved between on a seasonal basis. Their winter village was more hunting oriented than their summer and farming village. Agriculture was advanced. Both Tanama, who came from a society based upon hunting and gathering, and Einar were amazed and impressed by the relatively advanced farming methods and the yield they got out of the ground. The base diet for the whole camp was cereal supplemented by fish, fowl and wild game, which they all liked. Since there was no real inter tribe trade in animal furs, hunting was limited to what was needed, not what was possible. This meant they did not have to travel far to hunt, which was good. It kept them from problematic encounters with other tribes, and all the Scandinavians felt they had had enough of that for the time being.

The birth of Tanama's and Einar's first baby, a boy, was an incredible event to him. She asked, actually more or less demanded, that he be present, and the tribe allowed it since they were still outsiders and not formally absorbed into the tribe. The birth was something Einar would never forget. It instilled in him a sense of tremendous gratitude for Tanama, and bound them together in a way nothing else could have. Tanama seemed to have an easier delivery than what was usual for European women, though he had never directly witnessed a birth before, only heard stories about it. The baby was the wonder of the year for the tribe because he had red hair. This was so novel that after word got around, people from other tribes came to take a look. Tanama was tremendously proud of this, and basked in all the attention, saying the color was a sign from the gods that their union was blessed. Einar was not so convinced about that. He also worried a little about somebody trying to steal the baby, but soon realized such an event was highly unlikely here.

One of the main contributions of the Scandinavians to their new tribe was the introduction of bows and arrows. They were a simple type, made out of one piece of hard elastic wood up to six feet long. The power of these bows could not be compared to the composite bows used in Europe, but with limited tools it was the best they could do. And they were deadly enough.

When trouble came to them again, it was from an unexpected source. Macu had befriended a strong warrior named Red Bobcat. He came over to talk to her as much as possible. Espen was uneasy, but did not really know what to do. One day when Espen talked harshly to her, she answered him back, and he struck her down, hard. He knew he was doing the wrong thing, but was torn between a hopeless love and his pride as a man and warrior. When Macu recovered herself, she ran off. Espen did not pursue her, believing she would have to come back. But Macu did not come back. She ran over to Red Bobcat's tent. Espen knew he had to do something. He walked over to the tent and Red Bobcat was waiting outside. He refused to let Espen into the tent when he indicated through signs and words that he wanted the woman back. Others heard and saw what was happening and came over as the atmosphere grew hostile. Espen was grabbing for his sword when he felt his hand being held back by a strong hand. It was Thorfast.

"This is not the way or the time," he said. "Bring it up to the council around the campfire tonight."

Red Bobcat looked at Espen over the fire.

"Macu is not your woman here," he said. "She is not of your people. She hates you, despises you. I will be a good husband for her."

Espen looked like he was ready to bounce across the fire.

"Stop," Einar said to him, "or you will have us all killed. We are guests here. Let the elders decide. You have a good case." Leone translated what he said to the Indians. The old chief nodded. He looked tense, and obviously he did not want a fight either. They were often in conflict with their neighbors and other tribes, and unnecessary spilling of blood was not what they needed.

"We will talk about this in council tomorrow," he said, "you will be there." He nodded towards Einar.

The next day three elders, Espen, Red Bobcat and Einar met in one of the tents. Leone was there to help as an interpreter since the Northmen were not yet fluent in the language. Her husband (in a capacity Einar did not understand) also came into the tent. Einar felt sweat running down his back. He had to be determined, yet at the same time remember their rather precarious position. Espen started. After some appropriate opening phrases he said,

"I won this woman in battle far south of here. I took great risks to capture her. She would have died if not for me." He told the story of the rescue. "She belongs to me. When you make war, raid other villages, does not the warrior who captures prizes get to keep them?" The Indians nodded.

Red Bobcat stood up after Espen finished.

"You are not of our people, so our laws do not belong to you. This woman escaped from you. She came to me, so she belongs to me now." It was a short speech and to the point.

"We are guests in your village," Einar said, "and

have been treated very well. I do not know your customs, but in my land we do not take from guests, unless we are ready to fight." The challenge was unmistakable. Quiet descended on the small group gathered in the tent in the endless forest. Finally one of the old chiefs named 'He Who Sees like a Bird' opened his mouth.

"This is a difficult case. Both men have told the truth. If a wife goes back she will be punished, yet if a prisoner escapes she is now a guest. In cases like this, the rules are not so clear, and we will let men fight for their rights. In this case, if the men have to fight then let it be so. Tomorrow at the time when the sun is at its highest Red Bobcat, and Espen will fight."

Espen smiled. He was sure he could beat Red Bobcat using his superior weapons, but the old chief continued.

"They will each have the same kind of weapon, a club, and fight until one yields or dies." Einar was not happy about the war club. Espen would be unfamiliar with it and at a disadvantage, but there was little he could do.

That night was true hell for Macu. She wondered what she had done. She did not really know Red Bobcat. He seemed kind, but there was a certain streak of brutality in him as well. She would belong to Red Bobcat if he won, and if he lost she was sure she would be beaten badly by Espen. She decided the unknown would be better than the destiny she already knew.

The next day a clearing was made, and the men sat down in a circle with the women and children behind. The two contestants faced each other. They were both strong young men, each wearing only a loincloth and holding a wooden war club. Macu felt strange, afraid of either outcome, yet proud that two men would fight over her. For a young girl who had been dominated by others most of her life, this was a new sensation of power, of being desirable.

The two men faced each other in the clearing, slowly circling around, trying to reach out with the club, yet at the same time trying to block the other man's blows. Suddenly Espen got a full hit on Running Bear's lower left arm. All who were watching, which was pretty much the entire tribe, could hear the bone break. Macu felt fear grip her; it was as if somebody had poured a bucket of ice water into her stomach. It is only a matter of time, she thought, as did most of the others. Red Bobcat became careful now that he was hurt badly. His left arm was useless, but he was too proud to give up. Macu noticed the satisfied grin on Espen's face. He was like a big bear ready to finish off his prey. Suddenly he jumped over the fire to strike at Red Bobcat's broken arm, but he was too confident, too self assured. Red Bobcat managed to avoid the hit and swung his club full force into the side of Espen's head. For the second time the spectators could hear bone breaking, but now Espen just fell down on the ground, blood pouring from his ears. His face was frozen in a victorious grin, never realizing what had happened. Dead silence hung over the campfire. Then Macu got up and ran over to Red Bobcat who was on the verge of passing out. She grabbed his good arm and held him up. Einar and Thorfast recovered from the initial shock and stood up.

"It was a good fight," Einar said, "she is yours now."

He would miss Espen, in fact Espen had been one of the very few people that he called a friend, but there was no use crying over what had been. Macu looked at them both wide-eyed, realizing what had happened to her and that she belonged to another man.

Now everybody started talking about the fight, but Einar and Thorfast looked at each other, realizing they would be stuck here the rest of their lives. They had never had much hope of making it back to Vineland, but at least they had hoped. Now with only the two of them they knew any such venture would be close to completely hopeless. The question was whether they would be allowed to stay with this tribe. They would not have much of a chance on their own. Leone had told them earlier they could be adopted into the tribe, and would be given Indian names. So far he had resisted the suggestion, but now he really did not have much of a choice.

With this realization Einar took stock of his life. His life with Tanama was good, and the camp was peaceful, though they had heard from the few traders that came by, and also from related tribes that a new menacing tribe was pushing down from the North. It was called the Iroquois, and were mighty warriors operating in large groups. He made a decision, and discussed it with Thorfast.

"We have to become part of the tribe," he said, "it is our only way to survive." Thorfast had the same thought and readily agreed.

"I hope we don't have to get all the tattoos," he said. Some of the Indians had elaborate tattoos, while others had only a few scattered ones. Einar and Thorfast took their request to the council, who thought about it, then consented. The only requirement was that they participate in the indoctrination all the boys had to complete before they passed from boys to men.

Normally boys, age ten to fifteen, were initiated into manhood through the "huskanaw". This was a ritual that could last for nine months, a time of physical hardship, isolation in the forest, fasting, and medicine that would cause visions (or hallucinations). Boys were ceremonially taken to the forest from the village, and then returned as men. It could be a harsh ordeal and occasionally some boys did not survive, but a special bond was formed among those who survived. In the case of Thorfast and Einar, the elders of the tribe decided that one month of symbolic isolation was enough.

Gunhild and Tanama were a bit worried, but Leone comforted them saying it was mostly symbolic in their case, adding with a laugh that the hardest part would probably be to go without sex for a month. With this they settled down until the men came back. While they waited for the month to finish, Leone told them about their responsibilities.

"Here all women are queens, except for the prisoners," she said, "we own the fields, the children stay with you if your man leaves, and we can talk in community affairs. Even your children's lineage is followed through you."

"What is left for the man," Gunhild asked with a smile.

"He must hunt, clear the woods, maintain the house, make the fish dams, and most of all keep you happy day and night," Leone giggled. "It took me some time to get used to all this, and I guess I still have things to learn, but as women we are actually freer here than at home. We even trade for twice the amount of a man if we have to be ransomed after a raid."

The time in the forest was a strange experience for Thorfast and Einar. They were not supposed to communicate, but did so anyway. In some ways the experience was a blessing in disguise. They became familiar with their surroundings in a way which would have taken months otherwise, and they learned more about skunks, and other animals unique to the forests of North America. Mostly they hunted deer, but squirrels and other smaller animals were an important part of their diet. After the month had passed by, they had an appreciation for how rich this land was, not in gold but in life. They started to understand why nature was not wild to the Indians (they had no word for wild), the way it was to white men, but actually a part of life. Another thing which surprised them was that they became close friends. Later on in life they were never able to point to a specific event or moment, because it was a friendship that had evolved slowly, as the best friendships do. Men often try to rush friendship, but talk is a poor substitute for shared experiences and mutual trust. Quick and easy friendships rarely stand the test of time.

When the month was over, Red Bobcat and Leone's husband Black Beaver came and spent the last two nights with them. Red Bobcat's arm was still in a sling, but otherwise he was in good spirits. After an awkward start, both sides wondering if the other carried grudges from the fight, they found that they enjoyed each others company. They were close in age, and though from very different backgrounds, were all strong hunters and warriors. It was to become a friendship that would be remembered by the tribe long after they had all gone to the eternal hunting grounds.

As they walked out of the forest, Tanama and Gunhild came running up to them, Tanama throwing her arms around Einar's neck. This created much laughter, and, a little embarrassed, they pulled apart. Even in this country a warrior had to act in certain ways, and hugging his wife or girlfriend in front of the tribe was not among them.

Gunhild greeted Thorfast in a more subdued manner, hoping that he would acknowledge her and the baby as his own now that he was a full member of the tribe. Her relief when he did so was immense, like a giant burden lifted off her shoulders. Life without a man meant poverty in Norway, unless you had wealthy relatives. It was not quite the same here, but she sensed that she would have to marry somebody else if she did not have Thorfast. She was familiar with the looks of her new neighbors by now, but unlike Leone, she could not see herself living permanently with one of them, unless it was to save her children. For Thorfast their alliance meant two things. First Gunhild was still a very attractive woman. Second, it was almost as if he proved to himself that he was the equal of any Northman by taking her. In addition, none of the available Indian girls, cute as many of them were, appealed to him sexually. They were either too young or spoken for. He did not fancy ending up in a fight.

That evening the tribe held a big party, and Einar and Thorfast were officially admitted into the tribe. The old chief Four Crows gave Einar the tribal name Suckeu Moeakneu (Black Dog). Thorfast was named Teme (Wolf). Tanama became Taskemus (Mockingbird), and Macu was thereafter known as Chiskukus (Robin). They also learned that they should get some tattoos, but both were determined to keep that part to a minimum.

Einar felt great relief being back. Their places as members of the tribe were now secure, and even if he did not like to admit it, even to himself, he had missed Tanama tremendously. The evenings alone, without her warm body next to him, were empty. He was also at the young age where carnal relief was an important part of the night. Her obvious happiness seeing him warmed him and he gave her a big hug, though he knew it was not the Norse way to show your feelings so openly. The tribe was more accommodating to strangers than his hometown would have been if the roles were reversed. Typically small bands living in close contact with each other and nature are open minded out of necessity. Even strange behavior was accepted, as long as it did not hurt the greater interest of the tribe. European, so-called civilized manners, even by 11th century standards, become meaningless in the wilderness in a way only people who spend considerable time out in nature understand.

The next day a young man came up to Einar. He looked him proudly in the eyes.

"My name is Chihopokolis," he said, "I was the first to see your big canoe when you arrived the first time.

It was very exciting. I was afraid, but back then I was just a boy. I am a man now. Not one of those boys," he finished as he pointed towards some other boys playing a game in front of one of the tents. They were not much younger than him from what Einar could see.

"Good, you must have been very clever. We never saw you", Einar said, "I am proud to meet you Chihopokolis. In a way you were the first Delaware we met. I am glad you are one of the warriors here since you are obviously a good scout." He could see Chihopokolis was very proud to hear these words.

As he settled into camp life, Einar and Tanama shared a tent. Most of their neighbors had huts, but Einar liked the openness and fresh air of a tent. It would be colder in the winter months than a cabin or hut would be, but he never quite got used to the strange, foul smell in the huts. He had noticed similar smells in European huts, which was one of the reasons, even in Norway, he only used the cabin in the coldest winter months. Tanama would have preferred a cabin. It gave better protection in the winter, but it was not that important for her. Einar was her man and she would rather see him happy. If he was honest with himself, Einar would have understood there was another reason for not choosing a cabin. A cabin felt permanent, while a tent could move. He knew his chances of getting back to Norway were nonexistent, but he could not quite give up hope, not yet, not fully.

CHAPTER 9
A New Life

The moose was standing perfectly still, ears up, listening, sensing danger, but not reacting, not yet. In the early morning mist it looked almost as if it was floating on air. It was a beautiful and strange sight, but not one the hunters had time to enjoy. The moose heard a humming sound and tried to move away, but before it had taken the first step something bit into its side. Quickly spreading pain and numbness kept it from running. Expelling a final kick, it fell over on its side.

Einar walked up to the moose, looking at it proudly. His was a masterful shot in difficult wooded terrain, with the mist adding to the difficulty. The power of the arrow had buried it deep in the moose's neck, almost coming out on the other side. The three hunters with him nodded approvingly, and started to skin the animal.

"Your bow and arrow make us powerful hunters," Red Bobcat said.

A year had passed since Espen's death. The new tribesmen were, except for facial features and their slightly lighter skin color, almost indistinguishable from the rest of the tribe, dressed and armed the same way. Most of their European weapons had rusted or rotted away, and they kept the remaining ones stored and greased in animal fat in case of warfare. In the meantime they had been successful learning the ways of the native weapons. Einar kept the sword as a memento in his tent. It was a story unto itself, a memory of another place and another world, and a conversation piece. Friends would come and admire the sword and the strange material it was made of, and he would retell how he got it. For the three Scandinavians, the transition had been easier than they expected, and for the two Indian girls it was even easier. Life in these enormous forests with their abundant wildlife would have been a dream come true for hunters at any age. [It *has been estimated that there were approximately one million Indians in North America around the year 1000. This number would increase over the next few centuries, but even at the time of white immigration the population only reached something like five million. This number may be inaccurate, but whatever the actual number, it was small in relation to the size of the land. Warfare was rare, except for skirmishes in the Eastern Woodlands where farming was undertaken. Nomadic groups are generally small, and prefer to avoid confrontation unless it is forced upon them. Farming communities do not move so easily, and will fight to protect their land and food supply, moving only if the tribe encroaching on their area is too powerful.*]

The Scandinavians had also come to appreciate many things about Indian life that had not been so obvious from the outset. Their artistic skills, though different, were as good as European artistry. One day Tanama and Einar watched one of the older women make a plaited basket of hardwood splints with double rim hoops. She pounded a soaked log until the annual layers peeled off and she could use the splints. Einar sat down and wanted to try, but that created general laughter. This was woman's work. Indian woodworking was also of high quality. They made beautifully carved masks, as well as frames for drums and other instruments. Clothes were created with considerable effort, and were also of beautiful patterns and fit, and perfectly matched to the lifestyle. Tanama had a hard time learning some of the crafts, but she was young and determined to master the arts.

Despite the seemingly peaceful existence, this was a time of considerable turmoil in the Eastern Woodlands. Powerful tribes were moving in from the North and from the South. The Lenni Lenape had earlier been forced away from the Missouri country, and now this particular tribe was discussing whether to stay or move. The squeeze from both sides even created hostility between the Algonquian tribes themselves as game and land became scarcer. For a small band like theirs, warfare was a difficult path to choose. They did not have the manpower to absorb the losses that warfare inevitably created. The whole tribe was worried. The Shamans talked to the gods, but the gods did not answer.

Einar, Thorfast, Red Bobcat and Black Beaver had become close friends, often hunting together. As a group they were undoubtedly the best hunters and warriors in the tribe. With skilled hands they cut up the moose, saving almost every part of the animal. Normally Einar and Thorfast would only have preserved the meat like they used to in Norway, but from the Indians they had learned to devour every part, including intestines and other bits they had previously just discarded.

As the four hunters moved away from the carcass they became aware of human noises coming through the forest. They immediately went quiet, weapons at the ready, kneeling down, blending into the undergrowth. The group that came down the trail was large by local standards, maybe sixty members in all, including women and children. It did not look like it was on the warpath, since there were women and children among them. In fact upon closer scrutiny Einar realized there were fewer men than would normally have traveled in a group this size. It was also clear something had happened to them, many were wounded and they carried fewer possessions than would have been expected if they were moving camp. The group was obviously careful and on the lookout, but such a large group made noises anyway.

When they came close enough that words could be distinguished and faces made out, Red Bobcat and Black Beaver stood up.

"These people are Mahicans and our kin," they said to Einar and Thorfast, who also stood up and walked towards the group, hands open. They stopped at some distance, while some of the men from the other tribe approached them on the narrow trail. Einar saw that some of the Indians recognized each other as they greeted.

"We are leaving our camp." they said. "The Iroquois attacked us. They chased us from our home by the big river where our people have lived for as long as the old ones can remember. They had many warriors; more than ten men have fingers and toes. We fought very hard, but when they have two men for each of us there is only one end."

"How did you get away?"

"Our camp was right on the river. It is the only place where you can cross the river unless you walk for half a day. The crossing is very narrow. We who you see here came across before all was lost. The crossing is so narrow two men could block it. Three of our warriors stayed behind to delay or stop the enemy. The three warriors gave their lives so that we could escape, but half of our people were killed or captured. The Iroquois have strong medicine in their war clubs and they are many. They may follow us."

They offered to bring the group back to the camp. While Thorfast and Red Bobcat guided the strangers, Einar and Black Beaver would backtrack towards the raided camp to be certain the Iroquois had not stayed in the vicinity. The trail was easy to follow, but they were careful in case they would have stumbled upon a war band. After several hours walking fast they reached the bank of the river. The remnants of the great battle were everywhere. In addition to the broken tents, pots and other belongings, there were several dead Mahicans in sight, but no Iroquois.

'They must have taken their dead with them,' Einar thought. Three men were dead on the ground in front of them, obviously the three who had stayed behind to help the tribe flee, sacrificing themselves for the tribe. Along with other warriors they had been hacked to pieces. Einar had been told this was done so they would not be dangerous in the afterlife. Despite the inclination to bury them, they decided to leave the dead where they were. If the Iroquois returned they wanted to leave the impression that the fleeing tribe was far away, and not worth pursuing. Since the Iroquois had many prisoners to guard, there was little chance they would come back under any circumstances. However, if they realized the Mahicans were still in the area, there was a chance they would return after the prisoners had been brought to the Iroquois village. That was not a chance Einar and Black Beaver were prepared to take. With a last glance at the sad battle scene, a place where so many lives had been shattered, they turned home towards the camp. 'It is amazing,' Einar thought, 'even here in this big woodland people die in order to steal from others what they want. The mighty will always dominate the weak.'

The next evening around the great fire, the whole tribe met for council with the newcomers. Decisions were made that would affect the tribe for generations to come.

"We can fight them together," Red Bobcat said. "We cannot act like children who run away when others look upon us. We must be warriors of courage. With the help of our new bows and arrows we are the strongest." General grunts of acknowledgement followed his speech.

Einar was not so sure. He decided to speak out.

"If they have as many warriors as we have been told, as many as ten people have fingers and toes, then they far outnumber us." he said, "Though we may have some advantages, many tents will be empty by the end of the day if we fight, and many women will be without men. What will we do if other enemies come? To fight such a numerous enemy may be brave, but it is also useless. If anybody wants to stay here and fight, let them do so, but I think it is best to move to a peaceful home beyond the reach of the Iroquois. Red Bobcat is a brave man and a mighty warrior, but let us not risk the whole tribe in such a venture." He sat down.

It was quiet around the fire, except for the sound of burning wood. Tanama noted with satisfaction that most seemed to agree with Einar. Although he did not know it, his status in the tribe was approaching that of a chieftain. She was very proud that she shared her tent with such a man, so proud her eyes filled with tears and her heart almost left her chest. Besides, she did not want to stay and fight. Her own tribe had also fought against an overwhelming force, and failed. She did not want to risk her man, child and unborn baby in a hopeless cause. There were many stories regarding the Iroquois these days, and they all told of fearsome warriors. With pounding heart she stood up and spoke. The Delaware allowed the women to speak in council, though they did not encourage it.

"I come from a distant tribe," she started, stating the obvious. "We were also attacked by powerful neighbors. Our men were brave men, and good fighters, but the enemy had two warriors for each of ours. Nobody can win such a fight. Maybe one battle, but not many. I have heard that there are great forests to the north and west, across the mountains, where we can live in peace, and where the Iroquois cannot reach us. The game is plentiful, and men can see forever for there are few trees." She sat down. Part of her speech was a bluff to make the move more palatable, but the others could not know that. She felt Einar looking at her, and knew he had guessed the truth. Red Bobcat stood up again.

"There is wisdom in what has been said here today. I am not afraid to die, but this must be decided by the whole tribe." Though he could not admit it, he actually realized that he would rather move than face the enemy. He was not afraid, but neither was he suicidal, and the stories Einar, Black Beaver and the newcomers had told were enough to make any man think twice before he faced the Iroquois. Particularly when outnumbered.

An old man among the newcomers stood up.

"I am Spirit of the Skies." he started, "When I was a young man I was not Delaware, but Sauk." General astonishment followed his statement, only the very old had known his real background. "I was stolen by the Pottawatomie and traded to the Delaware with my mother. She told me of the land from where I came. It was by oceans that you could drink, at the edge of giant plains where huge animals grazed. The winters could be hard, but she told me few people lived there. There is plenty of space for new tribes."

"How far away is this place?" Einar asked. He was wondering if this could be close to Vineland, maybe a way to get home after all.

"It was very far," the old man said. "We would have to travel more than two summers."

Einar stood up.

"It may be the place where we can live in peace, the

place Tanama told us about," he said, not revealing his real motive. The chieftain from the newcomers stood up;

"If you decide to go, we want to go with you," he proclaimed. "We have lost many warriors, but together with you we can fight many enemies." There was nodding around the fire. The chanting grew to a staccato, "Leave, leave, leave." The old chief stood up again.

"We will follow the advice of Tanama" he said. "Though a woman she has seen such fights before. We will move across the big mountains to a new land, as soon as the corn has been harvested." Somebody threw more wood on the fire, and the shadows danced upon the trees as if ghosts were trying to pull them away from what had been their home for generations.

The next day they started preparations. Much had to be accomplished before they could be on their way. They made sleds, actually more of an X skid, for all their possessions. They wove baskets to carry corn. Without horses or other beasts of burden, moving camp was not easy. Everything had to be carried, and even fairly young children had to help. Over the next two weeks they gathered as much corn as they could possibly bring with them, then set out. Red Bobcat, Einar and Thorfast took turns scouting ahead of the tribe, mainly to avoid unnecessary confrontations. For weeks they traveled without incident, following trails west, meeting occasional natives, but only in a friendly manner. Some were uneasy at the first encounters, but when they made it clear they were just passing through they usually relaxed. The country became more and more hilly as they moved west, and after a few weeks they were all starting to wonder if these hills were endless. It was frustrating and tiresome to get to one summit, only to see another valley followed by another hill beyond. Every hill seemed only to lead to another hill.

Einar noted that, unlike in Norway, even the mountains were wooded. He had seen the same in southern Europe; the trees grew much higher up in the mountains. The nature was overwhelming for the small band of 200 people slowly making their way west, beautiful and monotonous at the same time. Another thing that struck the Northmen was how large the country was. Einar had seen endless areas before, in Russia, but here they imagined themselves on an island. Now he wondered if these hills went on forever, all the way to Odin's home. With fall coming the trees started to shift color, and as in previous years Tanama and Einar marveled at the red and yellow leaves against the hills. It made for a spectacular sight, and it never ceased to amaze them even though they had seen it before. Except for a few places, the hills were not steep, in the sense that they had no trouble walking them. The scouts always found animal or human trails to follow, and the weather stayed nice and warm for a long time.

"The gods favor us, they want us to settle beyond the mountains," Thorfast said. Einar was a bit amused that Thorfast had so completely absorbed the Indians spiritual beliefs.

They saw traces of other tribes, passed many campsites, and even some inhabited villages. They spoke in a similar dialect, so were somehow of the same ancestry as themselves. Some of the young warriors wanted to take over these sites, but Einar and the elders cautioned them.

"These villages are like the fingers of a hand," Einar said, "weak, but if we attack one they may band together and become like a fist." They always asked for information from the people they met, but few knew much about the land beyond their own tribe's hunting grounds. But when they encountered a tribe, calling themselves the Mingo people, an old man spoke at length to them about the areas ahead;

"I am Walking Bear," he said. "When I was young, I traveled far and wide, saw many strange sights, though none as strange as the hair on your face. What you have heard is the way things are. If you continue this way," (he pointed north-west) "you will come to lakes as big as oceans that may take many days to cross. Beyond that there are big hunting grounds, with huge animals." He also showed them some drawings on a deer skin, and talked about landmarks they should be on the lookout for. To Einar, the animals on his drawings looked like cows with enormous heads. All in all, it was an encouraging encounter, reinforcing their dreams of a new home, and verifying the stories the old man in their own tribe had told them when they left their original village.

The long hazardous journey was beginning to take a toll on everyone, particularly the old and very young. Some died on the way, and were buried in the traditional manner. The Indians had many gods, like the old Norse religions, and were great believers in ghosts and other supernatural phenomena. Their burial rituals had many symbolic aspects, and took too much time in Einar's view. He was eager to move on.

The cynic that he was, Einar did not put much faith in these beliefs, but he noted that all his Norse companions, not only Thorfast, were immersing themselves rapidly in the new "religion". 'So be it,' he thought, 'the old gods are probably not of much use in this country anyway.' At least they had not shown themselves to be very powerful so far.

Weeks came and went, but strangely enough the whole tribe was still in a good mood, despite the strain, about finding a new home in the abundant land with few trees. Winter was approaching rapidly now, and the tribe stayed in a large well sheltered valley that Red Bobcat had found. They built huts and tents, hunted game, and prepared themselves for the coldest months. Despite the protection of the surrounding hills against the most violent winds, Tanama had never experienced temperatures as cold as this before. It was like nothing she had even imagined. The cold wind would whip through a person like knives if one did not protect oneself. Luckily her new tribesmen and Einar showed her the skills necessary to survive and avoid frostbite. Her home in the southern forest never got cold, chilly maybe, but not cold. At night she would snuggle up to Einar inside the blankets and furs, feel the warmth from him go through her whole body, and more often than not end up making love. That was the only benefit she could see from the cold. At times she would wonder if the world would ever get warm again.

"Why does it get so cold?" she would ask.

"The days are short, and the sun does not have enough time to heat up the ground," was the best answer Einar could come up with.

However, even to Einar with his Nordic background, it felt extremely cold at times. The camp was at a higher altitude than they had lived before, and the cold was intense at night. He was used to the harsh wind, but during the day the sun felt warmer than it did during the winter in Norway. The days were not quite as short as in his hometown. One of the women got severe frostbite when she stepped through the thin ice of a lake. She later died in excruciating pain from the terrible wasting disease (gangrene) that followed. The tribe was helpless to save her, though they gave her some herbs to help ease the pain. The loss served as a reminder to all of them to be careful. She was "buried" up in a tree, there being no way they could dig into the frozen earth.

At the coldest part of the winter, in the month when the sun turns and starts to climb higher in the sky, Red Bobcat was out hunting when he detected movement. He dove behind a big rock, looking toward the sounds he heard. It was a big band of warriors, only two miles away, painted in wild colors. A war party, and they were on a course straight to the camp. It was lucky for the tribe that Red Bobcat was the one in this area, since he was generally known as the one with the sharpest vision in the whole camp. He slipped silently behind rocks as he ran the five miles back to the camp site, calling out warnings. Having become, over time, the war chief, Einar was the first person Red Bobcat spoke to.

"They will be here very shortly, we do not have much time," he said. Considering the situation, Einar called out for all the available warriors and others who could fight. They had discussed how to defend themselves often enough, so he lined up the warriors according to plan. The bowmen were in the front ready to shoot. He had also trained some of the old men, women and older children with bows and arrows to swell their meager numbers. Some of them were as good as the men, though not quite as powerful in pulling the bow.

"When they attack, wait to shoot your arrows until they are close enough that you know you can hit them," he said, "then run behind the rest and pick off any stragglers." Twenty minutes later the war party came running out of the forest amid loud screams and howls, only to be met by a hail of arrows. Two more rounds, then the bow men and women ran back. The attackers, thinking they had won despite their losses, lost all formation and charged, straight into the line of club wielding warriors. Despite their superior numbers, the attackers could not the break the line when the two groups crashed together. Einar's sword created terrible havoc with its strength and sharpness, 'The steel of Miklagard is truly a gift from the gods,' he thought. A steady stream of arrows also bore into the attacking tribe. After a few minutes they started to retreat slowly. Just as this happened, they were charged from the side by a small group of young warriors led by Thorfast. When it came to fighting a war, Einar trusted Thorfast more than the Indians. They were not used to organized warfare and easily lost all formation and forgot all plans. Under normal circumstances, tribal warfare were more like skirmishes, with the main objective to gain glory and prisoners, not extermination. But times were not normal. Einar's tribe could not afford to loose any fights, large or small. The charge from Thorfast and his warriors took the attackers completely by surprise, and the retreat became a rout. Tanama watched the fight from the tents. She was pregnant again, so did not take part in the fighting. She saw Einar with flying hair leading the warriors, and again she felt pride swell in her chest when she saw the attackers running away. They were still being chased by arrows.

"Look," she said to the other women with her. "The number of dead and seriously wounded are as many as six people have fingers. My husband is indeed the greatest warrior of them all." Her friends could only nod their consent.

The victory shouts and shrieks from the tribe were overpowering. Tanama felt herself being carried along with the excitement. The young girl "Wind-Flows" took a club from one of the men, ran over and clubbed one of the wounded enemy in the head, breaking his skull. Others were getting ready to follow suit when Einar shouted a powerful

"No, bring the prisoners here." They were all brought in front of him. Weak from wounds, afraid to die, yet trying to be courageous, they looked up at him with fear in their eyes.

"Do you understand my tongue?" Einar asked. "Why did you attack us?" The prisoners spoke what sounded like a heavy Algonquian dialect, not one of the Iroquoian dialects. One of the wounded answered, "We are Shawnee. You are on our land without our permission. These are our sacred hunting grounds."

"Then you will tell your tribe what I say." Einar

responded. "We were not aware these are your hunting grounds. We will not harm you. You will all go home to your camps." A mutter of general disbelief from his own tribe as well as from the prisoners greeted his statement. "You will tell your chiefs and elders there will be no more blood between us, though you attacked us. We will stay until the warm weather comes, and then we will leave this area. If you attack us again, many warriors will be killed. Now go."

The lead wounded warrior answered, "You are truly a great warrior with strong medicine, maybe from the hair in your face. I will tell our camp what you have said." The prisoners left, the lightly wounded helping the badly wounded along. Einar could never get over that all the Indians were so intrigued by his beard and long hair.

Some of Einar's warriors were unhappy with him.

"If we had killed them," Einar assured them, "the survivors and all of their friends and families would have attacked us again, soon, only the next time they would have been more cautious and not charged straight into our arrows. Now they may leave us alone. This has been bad medicine for them." His authority as the warrior chief was such that nobody argued against him for long. Besides, his friends Red Bobcat, Black Beaver and Thorfast supported him, and nobody wanted to alienate that group. Einar hoped he was right. If a new attack came, and it included the warriors he had just let go, he would surely loose all authority.

The victory dance lasted almost all night. It was a victory that would be told and retold over and over again by the tribe, the enemy becoming more numerous as the story was expounded year after year. With time it would take on mythical proportions and be weaved into the supernatural spirit world.

The next morning Einar told everybody to stay close to the camp, and he had five of the warriors on the lookout for trouble. As the hours passed by without any signs or sounds of strangers, they all started to feel more at ease, though they kept some lookouts posted several days after the battle.

Since they all had to stay close to the camp, Tanama spent a lot of time with the other women over the next few days. Usually she would mostly be with her own family and closest friends. Though technically a stranger, they all treated her with great respect. Tanama's tribe had been more advanced in some domestic areas, and she had taught them many new ways of making pottery, sewing, and cooking. Together with Gunhild and Leone, she was the woman most of the other women came to when they needed help. She was as happy as she could possibly be, though she was always afraid that Einar would long too much for his old life and wander off. She did everything she could to keep him, used every trick in a woman's book to make him want to stay. So far at least she had been successful. He took great care of their now three children, and that had dulled her fears. She did not think he would leave them, yet she was never completely certain, particularly when he and Thorfast talked in Norse. She asked Gunhild what they said, the little Norse she had learned earlier was by now forgotten, but Gunhild always said it was nothing, just ordinary men talk. Tanama settled for that, but she wondered if Gunhild told her the full truth or just what she wanted to hear.

Gunhild loved her new life. She would never leave. True this way of living was primitive. Her new neighbors would have scared the living daylight out of most of her previous Norse friends and family, with their face-paint, rings, tattoos, and fantastic haircuts. But overshadowing these curiosities was the all important fact that she was now free, free from violence, alcoholic family members, hunger and poverty. The memories of Norway, Geir and her old family were now but a distant and unpleasant memory, one she tried hard to forget. She got along very well with Leone and Tanama, and also with their husbands.

Thorfast was happy as well. Like Gunhild, he was free. Even better, he who had been but a work "animal," was now a valuable member of the tribe. Never mind that they were a strange looking lot. Gunhild and he had a good life together. They had grown to love each other, and were bound together by unhappy memories from a land and a time far, far away.

In the spring the tribe took down the camp and continued northwest. Before they left, some members of the tribe voiced their desire to stay.

"It has been a peaceful year," Painted Face said. A short argument followed, but again Einar carried the day through sheer willpower. On the day of their departure, what must have been a hundred warriors from other tribes emerged in front of the camp. They were painted which was not a good sign, Thorfast thought, but they did not appear to be threatening, just silently watching. When the Delaware's broke camp, one of the warriors came over to them and they recognized the wounded warrior from the winter battle. He greeted them saying,

"You have kept your word. You will travel in peace through our land." He walked away. Once again Einar's actions as leader had been vindicated. His prestige was growing.

The small tribe kept on going westward. At one stage they came upon a big river, big enough that they could use canoes. Thorfast was impressed by the way, and speed, in which the canoes were built, using wood and bark. They followed the river as far west as possible, but after a while there were too many places they had to walk. When they passed a place where the river split in two, both tributaries took a more south westerly course than they wanted. The additional weight of the canoes made it impracticable to keep them, so they left the vessels and continued their trek overland. The forest was not so dense anymore. There were fewer hills, and even fewer signs of human activity. They considered settling several places, but something always held them back—signs of other tribes, lack of fresh water, or ground that would not support agriculture or would require too much work to clear. Finally they came to an enormous freshwater lake, big as the ocean. Thorfast tasted the water.

"It is not a real ocean, no salt." He said. Einar knew they had followed a northwesterly course most of the time, and finally had to admit to himself that he was as far, or even farther, from Vineland as he had been when they started their westward trek. He just could not give up the dream of returning to Norway, and had hoped that this ocean was somehow connected to the

Atlantic. The fact that it consisted of fresh water proved otherwise.

Strange things started to happen, signs from the gods perhaps. One day they passed through an abandoned village. It was a strange ghostlike place, and had obviously been abandoned in a hurry, evidenced by all the items left behind. Yet there were no sign of a battle. As they searched through the village, they heard strange sounds coming up from a well-like hole in the ground. It was too dark to see what was down there, and after some deliberations Thorfast was lowered into the hole with a rope. As he descended he realized there was something alive down here. He felt flashes of cold fear going down his spine. Was it a human, an animal, or something worse? He reached the bottom before he knew what he would do. As his eyes adjusted to the dark, he could see the outline of rocks, and on them a living form. With the war club raised he slowly approached it. Suddenly the "thing" let out a high pitched scream and lunged forward. In a second Thorfast found himself striking out in all directions from sheer fear. The thing in front of him went limp, and fell to the ground. Thor stood still a few minutes, breathing heavily, slowly becoming aware of the shouts of concern from above.

"I am fine," he shouted back, and went over and felt the thing. The first thing he put his hand on was a breast, and with tremendous relief he realized it was a woman, not a monster. Quickly securing her with ropes, he signaled for the others to haul them up. The sight of the two of them on the surface caused more than a little consternation. The young woman, probably in her late teens, was skinny and undernourished. She had been hit in the head by Thorfast, but apart from her head wound did not look seriously hurt in any way. However, it was her looks that caused the consternation. Her skin was light when compared to the Indians, and her features European but with heavy lips. After the initial shock, some tribesmen wanted to kill her, out of fear of the unknown. Thorfast, however, objected to this. Her predicament was too much like what his own had been. When she came too they tried to talk to her in different Indian dialects, and it turned out she only knew a few words in what they believed was Iroquois, which unfortunately none of them were very good at. They tried Norse, and even some Anglo-Saxon words that Thorfast knew, but to no avail. Thanks to the sign language they learned, however, that she had drifted across the sea from the north as a child, been shipwrecked, rescued by an Indian tribe and subsequently traded between tribes. With poor language skills, and the fact that she only remembered parts of her childhood experiences, Einar and Thorfast nevertheless concluded she, or her parents, were from Europe. They had not heard about other European settlements, but wondered if other settlements had existed in the past. The girl was quickly absorbed into the tribe, and her unusual looks made her into a local celebrity. If anybody did not treat her the way she liked, she told elaborate strange tales in a foreign language, which were usually enough to scare most people from bothering her again. [*In modern times, DNA testing has showed European DNA among Indians in Canada*]

They followed the coast north. The new woman joined them as a member, not a prisoner, on Thorfast's insistence. He knew what enslavement was and did not want to impose it on others. Since the girl and the fresh water ocean were considered good omens, a certain excitement spread among tribe members. Einar, Black Beaver and Thorfast were still scouts. Red Bobcat did not join them as often anymore. He had marital problems. Macu was a troubled woman. Red Bobcat understood her ordeal had left an invisible scar on her. Nightmares and violent mood swings were the result. One moment she yelled at him, the next clung to him. He asked others for advice, but they could not help. At night Macu would let him make love to her, but only lay still, as if the whole experience was none of her concern. Macu needed the kind of mental help that was still centuries in the future. Leone had gone through much of the same experience, but had been able to put it behind her, maybe because she was older and a more stable nature. Whatever the reasons, Red Bobcat was unable to help her. Another problem was that they did not conceive any children. For an Indian, a son or at least a daughter was one of the main things in life. Macu had been pregnant twice, but miscarried both times. In cases where couples did not conceive, it was not unusual for them to "adopt" orphans, children from brothers or sisters or from families with too many children. However, with Macu's mood swings, none in the tribe were willing to give her any children to care for, afraid of what might happen to that child. Understandable as it was, it aggravated her mental problems. Eventually she became hateful toward Tanama and Leone. Why were they doing so well? Both had three children now, while she was stuck with a pitiful man. As the trek continued she isolated herself more and more, and eventually even her friends turned away. Macu was haunted by her experiences—the war which had made her a prisoner, the wait to be sacrificed by the Maya's, the unexpected rescue, the ordeal on the boat. She had felt a brief surge of power when two men fought over her, only to realize that her life did not change much even if the outcome was what she had hoped for. Red Bobcat could not handle the difficulties. He was a bright man, but his limited experiences did not guide him in this situation. He and the other tribe members started to believe an evil spirit possessed Macu, and all they could hope for was that it would leave her. They wanted the medicine man to help her, but Macu declined help in such a way there was nothing anyone could do. The medicine man was secretly relieved. He sensed her problems were on a different level from the ones he usually dealt with, and rather than risking failure, he let Macu drift further and further away into her private hell.

CHAPTER 10

A Freshwater Ocean

The tribe followed the coast for two more weeks looking for a new home. Finally, the scouts came back and told of a rich fertile land ahead. Upon reaching it, they all felt this was it, their new home. To Einar it felt almost like a long lost home. It was by a small bay, heavily wooded on one side and with rich soil. On all sides except the bay side it was ringed by boulders and small hills, forming a natural and defendable barrier. This also made it hard to see the camp unless you were close, and the water created an escape route as well as source for food. They did not see any signs of other camps around. Another factor in their decision to stay was the tribal bands they had recently seen. They were smaller than the tribes they had encountered in the vast eastern woodlands, and most of them seemed to be nomadic rather than farmers. Combined with the war advantage the bow and arrow gave them, they felt confident they could defend themselves and their fields.

That night a huge fire lit up the forest. All the adults gathered, each giving his opinion about whether to stay or not to stay. The Indian tribes, like the Northmen, practiced a form of democracy, at least among adult men. Any free man could say what he wanted, share his opinions and stand his ground without being intimidated. Free women, if not exactly of equal standing to the men while in council, could also contribute to important decisions, their voices heard in both societies. For Einar, the campfire council was similar to the "Ting" [*a word which today is synonymous with Parliament in Scandinavia*] that the Norse practiced. During the Ting period, peace reigned and any free man regardless of wealth could speak his mind, at least in theory. The discussions around the campfire were similar, and when all was said and heard, most of the adults wanted to stay.

With the decision out of the way, the party started. They had been traveling for almost two years, so a new home was most welcome. It was like nothing Einar, Gunhild and Thorfast had ever experienced.

They had seen previous Indian festivities often enough, but nothing like this celebration for their new home. Most clothes were shed before the dance, and consequently the men and boys were mostly dressed in loincloths when they started. The women had deerskin dresses. The dancing around the big fire followed a familiar pattern, circling the fire in a counter clockwise direction. Einar never understood why that was so important, but he accepted it as probably another custom ordained by the gods. The constant beat of the drum accompanied by rattles was supplemented by a man singing for the women to come out, which they did after awhile. Einar looked for Tanama among the dancers. She was one of the tallest of the Indian women and easy to recognize with her slightly different features. He almost felt electrified when he saw her, lightly dressed which meant he could enjoy the sight of her beautiful bronze skin. The smell of sweat from the dancing bodies combined with the constant drum of the music, the shadows from the fires dancing on the big trees and reflections from water all blurred together and transported him to an almost surreal world. The dancing continued for hours into the night, until people started to drop out from sheer exhaustion. Watching Tanama with the other women dancing around the fire, it was impossible for Einar not to be aroused, or not to do something about it. Finally, he lifted her up and carried her into their tent, her small hands clasped around his neck, her lips pressed against his.

Over the next few weeks a permanent camp was established. Land was cleared, and cabins and tents erected. It was summer, and they felt the heat more keenly in the relative openness of the new settlement than they had in the forests from where they came. The ample opportunities for hunting and fishing brought everybody back to health, even those who had encountered problems following the long trek west. The men ranged far and wide, and though they encountered other tribes, no hostility was encountered. The land was just too big to fight over. A portion of the tribe moved a few miles inland and set up their camp there. They were close enough for mutual protection, yet far enough away that maintaining the food supply would be easier.

In late summer, Einar, Thorfast and Black Beaver agreed to survey to the west. They traveled for days and weeks. With their feel for the terrain and landmarks, they were never afraid of not finding their way back to the camp. The land was not as hilly as they were used to on the East Coast, allowing them to see over long distances.

One night, just as they were going to sleep under the first full moon on their trip, Black Beaver touched the feet of his two companions.

"Look," he said. "It is one of the spirits." Fear running down their spine, Einar and Thorfast fought an urge to run away from the sight Black Beaver pointed out to them. An enormous animal, bigger than anything they had seen, stood near their sleeping spot—as their night vision got better they realized there were several in the vicinity. The men did not dare to move but waited for daylight. It was long in coming, feeling even longer due the presence of these ghosts. As the sun came over the horizon, their fear abated, as fear usually does when met with daylight. Einar realized the animals looked somewhat like huge cows or horses, but each had a hairy head much larger than they had seen on any animal before. He suddenly remembered the drawings the old man had shown them the first year of their trek. At that time he had thought they were just bad drawings, but now he realized the old man had drawn what was a very good impression of these animals. They had met their first buffaloes.

Their courage had now returned, and with it their hunting instincts. Black Beaver flexed his bow, and let the arrow fly. It hit the huge animal just behind the front leg, but was not powerful enough to bring it down. The small herd stampeded away, the wounded animal with it. Both Thorfast and Einar shot arrows after the wounded animal as it raced on, and both hit it. It fell behind the herd, severely wounded but still outrunning the humans. In awe of the sight, the trio decided to follow the herd's trail. After many hours tracking, they came upon the wounded animal, standing still and shivering. The rest of the herd was long gone. As they approached the wounded beast, it used its last reserves to charge them, but it was weak and the men avoided the charge with ease. The animal stopped, panting and exhausted. The men charged it, clubbing it with their stone axes. Initially this had little effect, but soon the big animal keeled over from the constant barrage of blows. With a final lunging with its head, which caught Black Beaver's hip, it died with a final gasp of air. They stood around it, proud to have caught the prey, tired from the hunt, wondering what to do next. They started parting it with their knives, which was heavy and tiresome work with stone tools. The hide extremely tough to cut, and after a while they simply gave up.

"This will take more time than we have," Thorfast said, "let us take the parts we have cut off and return to tell the tribe about this." Leaving the carcass for the ever present four-legged scavengers, they started back to the camp, still wondering about the animal.

"I wonder if there are other secrets out on these fields," Einar said, "or dangers, people we have not yet met. How far do you think these fields stretch?"

"When I was a young boy, I heard stories of these plains." Black Beaver said, "They go on forever, all the way to a big ocean."

"How do you know that?" Thorfast asked.

"The old ones told us so," was the answer.

When they started to walk back, it soon became clear that Black Beaver's hip needed to heal, the wound was deeper than they had initially thought. The men stayed put for a few days, enjoying buffalo steaks. Einar passed the time by taking small walkabouts. On one of these he had the strangest experience he would have for many years. He found a stone with Norse runes [*letters*] carved into it. It told the story of how some Norse traders sailed south from Norway and then ventured west across the ocean. From the moss on it, he realized it was many years since it had been inscribed. He was very excited and added his own little inscription. It gave him something to do, and he was wondering what happened to the people who made the inscription. Maybe there was some connection between this place and Greenland or Vineland. Not being a great speller, he knew he would get some of the spelling wrong, but took solace in the thought that later generations might find the stone and allow him to be remembered as important to the Norse. When he told Thorfast about the discovery, he showed no interest. He did not fancy meeting Scandinavians, he had seen more than enough of them in the past.

Black Beaver healed faster than expected, and Einar had to make his story on the stone very short indeed. Nevertheless, he enjoyed the thought of somebody finding the stone in the future. It was not to be, but another stone would be found, called the Kensington stone by later generations, and it was destined to become the source of much controversy.

When the men returned, they found the whole camp roaming about. Macu had disappeared. They joined the search for her. Hours went by without anybody seeing her, or finding any trails marked by her. It was getting dark when, on a hunch, Leone looked down a ravine. She saw clothes on some stones and climbed down. With a pumping heart, she rounded the last boulder and found Macu. She was beautiful, lying on her back, staring up into the sky. In death her face was peaceful, a peace she had not experienced in life. Under different circumstances, she might have lived a full life, and maybe having a child could have saved her. But life did not give her a child, it gave her only hardship, and in the end it was more hardship than she could handle.

They buried her in the traditional manner, sorry to see her go despite her difficult disposition. Tanama was particularly sad, and tears welled up in her eyes. Macu had never been a really close friend, but she was the last link to her former life. To her dying day, Tanama would wonder if Macu had committed suicide or fallen into the ravine, and if there was anything she could have done to save her. Red Bobcat missed Macu, but privately he felt this was the best resolution. She had been too troubled, and now he was free to marry again, and to get what every warrior craved, a son.

The scouting trip had been a great success. Einar wanted to explore further, but it was too late in the year, and a follow-up trip would have to wait. Now it was time to hunt and harvest nearby in preparation for a rough winter. The winter proved even harder than before, the wind and high humidity meant that some days they did not even venture outside the tents and cabins. As it was they were well stocked with food and firewood, and in the long evenings the various clans would gather around the campfire and tell stories or play games. It was a peaceful existence, and rare were the days when Einar felt bored. At times they had to go out and remove snow. The snowfalls were short, but the amount of usually wet snow that came down in a day or two amazed them all. At other times the sun shone and much of the snow disappeared. Einar guessed their closeness to the lake had something to do with the weather pattern.

CHAPTER 11

The Canoe Trip

The following spring, Red Bobcat and Einar set out on a canoe trip. They wanted to see what was along the lake coast, both as a precaution against potential enemies and out of sheer adventure. The sky was clear, there was no breeze, and it was perfect for canoeing. Over the next few days, they paddled carefully along the coast, marveling at the size of this lake which was surely as big as an ocean. Einar knew about large oceans south of Norway, but they all had salt water. Because this giant lake was fresh water, he discarded any connection between it and the Atlantic. The men experienced how suddenly the weather could change in this region, with sudden drops in temperature and bursts of wind coming seemingly from nowhere. All in all, Einar felt happy and exhilarated. A sea voyage, even in a small canoe, was in his blood, and he enjoyed seeing new lands.

Red Bobcat was good company, and he needed to talk to Einar to ease his heart.

"I am sorry I killed your friend Espen," he said. "But my desires for the woman were too great for me to see clearly."

"It was not your fault," Einar answered. "Such things happen when men's feelings grow too strong. Espen felt the same way you did. He was a man, not a child, and men must finish what they start. He was a good friend and sensible in most things, but he brought these problems onto himself. If he had treated Macu better, then maybe she would not have been stalked by the dark spirits." Red Bobcat nodded, there was nothing more to be said. He changed the subject.

"You told me once of a great battle. Were many warriors killed?"

"It was in a far off place called Stiklestad, and yes, more hunters were killed than there have been people in any of the tribes we have met," was the answer. Red Bobcat was quiet.

"A lot of honor must have been won that day," he finally said.

"No," Einar answered quietly, "nothing was really

won, just suffering and misery. Wives were left without husbands, children without fathers. It would have been better if the battle had never been fought. The king should have allowed the people to follow their own gods, and not force them to believe in his." Einar's answer surprised himself as much as it did Red Bobcat, but it showed how much he had changed mentally. Here, among these so called "primitive" people, he had gained an appreciation of the value of life itself, and realized that to die in an attempt to change others' beliefs, or take their properties, were not worthy causes.

"Do you think your people will come here?" Red Bobcat asked.

"I do not know, but I fear so. If they do many battles will be fought, and many warriors will die. Let us hope they will never find us."

With this they became quiet, both lost in their own thoughts. For Einar, it was almost like he had a vision of what the future would bring. He realized that the Indians would never be able to resist a large scale European attack. They were just too few, and their weapons inferior to the iron swords and shields used by the white men. It would be even worse than he thought as more advanced weapons would render the Indians without any chance whatsoever. But that was all hidden, far into the future. He knew it would not happen in his lifetime, but he feared for his children and following generations.

The next morning they went hunting. There was less wildlife, but they got two rabbits, always good and nutritious food. That afternoon a sudden wind burst blew them far out onto the lake. They thought they saw land on the other side, but not being sure they decided to leave any venture across the lake to a later expedition. Eight days after departure, they noted a large settlement ahead of them. They approached carefully but openly, hands outstretched. It was quiet as they approached. They felt uneasy. Suddenly about fifteen braves jumped them before they had a chance to prepare weapons or run away. After a brief fight they were overpowered and tied up. The clothing they wore was stripped away from them. They had met the Kickapoo.

Sore from kicks and strikes, but not seriously hurt, they were thrown into a tent where there was already another prisoner. He looked dazed and had problems focusing his eyes. It was obvious he had been captured after a fight, and had been knocked hard in the head. From his slurred babbling and uncoordinated eyes, they first thought he had a concussion, but soon realized that he had been there some time and probably had brain damage. Because the Kickapoo thought he had been possessed by an evil spirit they had not killed him outright, afraid that would unleash the spirit and make it possess another person. Einar could understand some of the words the kickapoo said, so the languages had to be related, yet there was enough of a difference he realized he would not be able to explain the mix-up to them. They were dressed mostly in deerskin, many beautifully decorated, though Einar was not in apposition to enjoy that right there and then. He could also see that the Kickapoo were farmers like them, and seemed to live in huts. If they could somehow communicate with them, the Kickapoo would have much to teach them about the area. Unfortunately reasoning was not something their captors were ready for as yet.

"We will have to run the gauntlet tomorrow, and we will not survive." Red Bobcat said. The Indian tribes he had encountered had many customs that struck even a man with Einar's background as cruel and barbaric. For example extended torture of prisoners, rituals like letting prisoners run the gauntlet with the tribe clubbing them along the way or tying down captured women and cutting them up piece by piece, often with strong sexual overtones. He knew that many of these customs had their roots in religious and tribal traditions, and were considered almost honorary to the prisoner. With his lack of religious fervor he nevertheless considered them crazy and ridiculous. Of course that was not something he would share with the others, even Tanama or Thorfast. He had carefully tried to stop some of these customs in his own tribe, but with limited success. Only when he could offer an understandable alternative would he prevail. At times, the tortures had made him so uncomfortable he walked into the forest to avoid the whole ceremony. Luckily there were few instances where torture occurred, and when they happened few noticed him leaving, and he did not interfere. After all it was even worse in the torture chambers in Europe where they built machines to aid in the torture of captives. His own people also enjoyed torture when raiding, so what happened here was not exactly a novelty to him. It just felt extra bad in these beautiful forests and hills, the contrast between the breathtaking scenery and the misery so striking. Even Tanama had a cruel side he did not fully understand, or even try to understand. She was wonderful to the children and the rest of the tribe, but to outsiders she could be fierce and unforgiving. They were both originally outsiders to the Delaware's, but she seemed to forget that at times. Einar was a practical man. A prisoner could be sold, or used as a bargaining chip. Outright torture and slaughter only led to retaliation and blood feuds. If necessary, he would kill a prisoner, but quickly. He took no pleasure in watching agony. The good part was that the tribes were so thinly spread out warfare was very limited. [*With the increase in the Indian population over the next few centuries warfare would increase, but only with the advent of the white men and their weapons, would the killings reach the crescendo of European warfare.*]

Einar knew Red Bobcat was right about not surviving the gauntlet. They had to escape before morning, but how? He wondered why they had been attacked outright. This was very unusual among the tribes. Looking through the tent opening, he noticed that several warriors had cuts and bruises. They had landed in the middle of a tribal war, but he knew he would not be able to convince their captors they had made a mistake. Their captors' bloodlust and thirst for revenge was too great. He had noticed before how people, Indians or Europeans, could reach a level of blood-thirst which transcended reason and would run its course until it burned out. Human nature after all, did not seem to differ too much from continent to continent.

Only one guard was left in the tent, but with their hands and feet tied there was no way Einar and Red

Bobcat could overpower him. Morning came, and they were still no nearer to a solution, and started to accept their fate. Some braves came into the tent and pulled them out into the open area in the middle of the camp. Trying to keep his emotions in check, Einar was wondering how they would be killed. However, the Indians had other prisoners they wanted to dispose of first.

A young woman was led out naked, and tied down spread eagle on the ground. She was pale with fear, her eyes bulging out. Tears flowed, streaking her face with sweat and dirt. An old woman came forward, took out a sharp shell and proceeded to cut off bits and pieces of her skin, including her nipples. She then put them in the victim's mouth and held it shut until she was forced to swallow. A little later a young brave came forward and cut off her eyelids off so she could not close her eyes. The torture became a blur to Einar after that, and he was sick to his stomach, but Red Bobcat watched intently as if hypnotized by the spectacle. When the young woman finally died following hours of torture, Einar was as relieved as he had ever been in his life. He was simultaneously appalled with the episode and grateful he hadn't revealed his own emotions in a noticeable way. He had been close to vomiting, and fear was not something he wanted to show in this situation. It would just make things worse.

Following the torture of the woman, a brave captured from another tribe was tied down between four bent trees, which were then released, pulling the brave apart to much shouting. Einar and Red Bobcat had been largely left alone, only receiving occasional kicks and spits from passing Kickapoo. Finally some braves approached them, and Einar started to prepare himself for death. He had seen it often enough, but now it was his own and that certainly made things different. But luck was with them this day, and instead of taking them into the center of the crowd, the braves dragged the captives by their feet back into the tent. Their bloodlust had been satisfied for that day. Night descended, and Einar dreaded what the next morning would bring. It would be weeks before they were missed, so rescue was highly unlikely.

Suddenly Einar noticed that their pack was in the tent, and nobody had gone through it properly, only taking the food. He felt his heart beat faster as he remembered that his last remaining European knife was there. He slowly inched his way over to the pack. When the guard looked at him, he indicated that he needed movement in his arms and legs to get the blood circulation going again. The guard laughed, but let him roll back and forth. After an hour he was close enough to the pack to put his head on it as a pillow. But the guard kicked it away, laughing again. Einar cursed silently from frustration, and then started crawling back and forth again. This time when he got to the pack he decided to pretend he would use his hands to push it to the side. Sweating more from fear than from exhaustion, he felt inside the pack. Thank you Odin, the knife was still there. He almost sighed from relief, then carefully grabbed the knife, hiding it in his hand. The guard was no longer paying particular attention. None of the weapons he was used to would have been possible to hide in a hand,

and he had never seen a metal knife before, consequently he was not worried about Einar hiding anything in the pack. Einar had to wait for the camp to go quiet. When it did, and the guard's eyes were getting heavy as well, Einar carefully rolled to his back, and started to cut through the ropes tying his hands, all the time hiding what he was doing under his back. After they had been cut, he repeated the maneuver with the ropes tying his feet. .

The next hour felt like an eternity. Einar had to pretend he was sleeping, and at the same time the sensation of the blood circulation returning to his limbs made him want to scream. When the camp was finally fully quiet, the guard had also dozed off, though he was not really sleeping. Einar knew he would have to kill him silently so he could not alert the camp. In addition, they would need time to wait for Red Bobcat's feet to regain their circulation or he would not be able to run. Einar watched the guard, and when his head rolled to the other side, Einar was on him like a tiger, one hand closed over his mouth, the other pushing the knife right into the guard's ribs. It got stuck, and the Indian bit Einar's hand, getting ready to scream. With a strength born out of desperation, Einar freed the knife, then plunged it in again, between the ribs into the heart. The Kickapoo went limp.

Einar breathed so heavily he thought the whole tribe would wake up, but nothing moved. With effort, he got up and freed Red Bobcat, who had awakened during the fight. After waiting for Red Bobcat's circulation to return, they left the tent. Silently they snuck down to the lake and could not believe their eyes when they saw their own canoe. They did not have time to smash the other canoes, and it would also have been too noisy, but Einar used his knife to cut holes in the nearest ones.

Just as they were about to set off, they heard a shout from camp followed by screams. They jumped in their canoe as fast as they could and paddled off with their captors in hot pursuit. The Kickapoo jumped into their canoes, and screamed more as they discovered the cuts in some of them. But three canoes with about twenty warriors managed to follow the escaping captives. The Kickapoo were much faster, having more rowers per boat, and Einar and Red Bobcat were exhausted from not eating or drinking properly for days.

After half an hour with the pursuers steadily gaining ground, Einar and Red Bobcat realized there was no way they would be able to lose them. What would they do now? Somewhat belatedly, they checked to see if the Kickapoo had taken their weapons out of the canoe, and a quick glance around told them most everything had been removed. Well, better to die fighting than tied down to a stake, thought Einar. But then he noticed something half hidden under an old deer skin—their bows and arrows, apparently overlooked by the Kickapoo women who had emptied the boat and did not know what they were.

"You paddle!" Einar said to Red Bobcat as he got the bow ready. The enemy was only 50 to 100 yards away. He placed an arrow in the bow, aimed carefully and shot. It went through a Kickapoo arm, then hit another in the chest but apparently neither was seriously hurt. The enemy canoes stopped momentarily, started paddling again, but hesitated a second time. Even with only Red Bobcat rowing, the escapees had gained ground. One canoe turned back towards the camp, but the two canoes in which nobody had been hurt pressed forward again, faster this time, quickly coming closer, obviously thinking they could overwhelm the fugitives before they had time to shoot more than a couple of arrows.

The escaping captives were moving very slowly now. Red Bobcat was totally out of breath. As their pursuers came within range, Einar readied another arrow and shot it. But he missed, only striking the boat and punching a harmless hole. He would have time for just one or two more arrows before they would have to fight hand to hand, and he swore he was going to sell his life dearly. The next arrow flew, and this one hit a Kickapoo straight in the chest. He fell backwards, and tipped the entire canoe over, emptying everyone into the lake. Einar and Red Bobcat roared with triumph. Einar readied his last arrow, but the last Kickapoo canoe turned around. They had had enough.

They continued slowly until they found a small deserted inlet, and stopped for the night. They were too exhausted to keep watch, so just hid the canoe and collapsed on the ground. The odds of anybody finding them were remote under any circumstances. They woke to a beautiful day. Elated as they were to be alive, any day would have been beautiful. After eating some berries and drinking plenty of water, they felt good. Then they both noticed it at the same time. They were being watched!

"Not many, maybe one or two." Red Bobcat

whispered out of the corner of his mouth. First
pretending nothing was wrong, they then charged the
bushes on a command from Red Bobcat. After a short
fight, they found they were holding down a young girl
about fifteen years old. She was scared, with tears in
her eyes. Just like them she was completely naked. The
two men relaxed, then started laughing, at their own
behavior, until finally they were roaring with laughter.
The girl looked at them, still afraid but also wondering
what was happening. They finally spoke to her. She was
difficult to understand but said she was from the Sauk
tribe. She had been moving with her family and some
kin when the Kickapoo attacked, killing her parents and
capturing her brother and sister. Though initially
captured she had escaped during the night in a stolen
canoe. The Kickapoo had searched for her, but she had
sunk the canoe with stones, and believing she had
paddled far away the Kickapoo had stopped searching
after a few hours. It was just a week ago, and they
realized the two people they had witnessed being killed
in the Kickapoo camp were most likely her family. Einar
told her they were dead, but not how they died. She had
survived on berries, and apart from being hungry was in
good shape. The men got the canoe ready and brought
the girl with them.

"I will buy her from you," Red Bobcat told Einar,
since he owned half of her.

"Agreed," Einar said. "Two beaver skins and one
rabbit." He would have been just as happy to give her
away, but Red Bobcat would have had to give him a gift
in return, and this friendly bargaining made it easier.
The young woman was quite attractive, if not
beautiful, and Red Bobcat needed a woman. In her

circumstances, she could not do much better than to become his wife, being a prisoner, and an age when most girls married. The girl realized what was going on from the words and signs she could understand, and since Einar's pale skin scared her she told herself she got the better deal.

The men decided to return home, but needed to consider how to avoid the Kickapoo tribe. Even if they rowed at night, they would have at least one or two days when they had to hide, and their enemies would be looking for them. A canoe could be seen over long distances. An overland trek was a possibility, but it would be a long hazardous journey.

"We will sleep in the boat, far out at sea, and paddle day and night," Einar finally said. Red Bobcat and the young woman both looked at him as if he was crazy.

"I can steer by the stars and the sun," he said. Einar believed that this body of water was an enormous lake, and so, even if the wind carried them, they would not be lost at sea but instead hit land at the other side. After a short but heated discussion, Red Bobcat conceded. He was still unhappy, but could not offer a workable alternative.

Einar rigged the canoe with a cover made of branches to protect them from the sun. They found there was room for one person to lie down and sleep with the other one or two rowing. In the late evening they set off. Einar recalled another departure when he had sailed straight out from land. It seemed like an eternity ago. Hopefully they would be more successful this time.

As soon as they were out of sight of land, they turned almost due south. Einar was in a good mood since to him this was almost like a sea voyage, but his two companions were frustrated. On an open water voyage like this, there was a feeling that the boat was not moving at all. Particularly in a small canoe, the feeling of being alone in the world with no hope was intense. They paddled slowly all through the night. The gods were on their side, since there was very little wind and much quiet. Einar's thoughts wandered off again. He was thinking about all the twists and turns his life had taken. Smiling to himself, he was imagining what the looks on his parents faces would have been, if he walked in on them looking the way he did these days, loincloth and all. The silent breathing of his two companions half asleep was all he heard in stillness of the night. Then, suddenly, they were all there, his parents, his brother, the people on the Longship, the dead and the dying, men and women he had known in the past. He found he was freezing despite the warm summer breeze. He wanted them all away. It was too real, too frightening, but they did not go away.

"We are waiting Einar, waiting for you," the chorus was intense. At the same time, despite the presence of all these people, they left an intense emptiness in him. It was a last gasp of a life he once knew, of places he would never see again. They were so real, then a new face appeared, Tanama, she waved at him,

"Come home," she said, "come home to me." The others started to fade away in the background. With a nod he woke up, he had fallen asleep. He was so relieved about waking up he wanted to shout, but ended up just sitting there, thinking about the sight he had just seen. What did it mean? Was it a message from the gods, or just a nightmare from hell? He decided it was best to put the whole thing to rest. The gods had to speak clearer if they wanted him to act. It was a good thing he had held on to the paddle, for without it they would have been lost. Carefully he started paddling again. It would soon be Red Bobcat's turn to take over. The rest of his turn he concentrated on watching the surroundings, almost afraid to fall asleep again.

The second day was much harder. The sun beat down relentlessly, and the voyagers made little progress being tired and exhausted. The fact that there was no wind was in their favor, since they would not have been able to go against the elements. After a while they only paddled one at a time, discouraged by the endless blue sky and blue waves. Hunger crept in. They had berries and nuts for one more day, but no meat or other food. At least fresh water was no problem on this lake. Night came again, and their progress was still painstakingly slow. Heat exhaustion was affecting them all, and the girl had taken to just lying in the bottom of the boat. On the morning of the third day, they changed course to the southwest.

"We have to risk the shore, or we will die here," Einar whispered. They were out of food now, and were getting weaker by the hour. As they carefully approached land, tension was high. Had they passed Kickapoo territory? The morning fog made it impossible to see any distinguishing landmarks or features before they were quite close to the shore. Finally Red Bobcat broke into a big, if tired, smile.

"Eagle Rock," he said. It was a place they had stopped on their way north, and named after the eagle they spotted while they camped there. They were safe. Going ashore the three travelers immediately started to eat berries and grass, anything to quell the hunger in their stomachs. In the evening they even managed to catch a hare which was roasted. Life felt good again, and they had the first good night's sleep in five days.

A few days later they approached their own camp. Friends and families crowded around them as they told of their adventures. They were curious about the new tribe member. Some of the children, and a few others, started bossing her around, thinking she would have to do all the duties prisoners often did, like carrying water from the lake. However, a short word from Red Bobcat put a stop to that, and instead there were humorous comments regarding Red Bobcat, and single men and women in general. For Red Bobcat the trip was the biggest event of his life. He would forever tell his children, and later the grandchildren, how they had slept out on the ocean, and how Einar had managed to steer the boat in the dark, just looking at the stars.

Around the campfire that night the tribe made some decisions. One was that they all had to be in groups of at least four when they ventured northwards toward the Kickapoo territory. Secondly they would send a group to meet with the Kickapoo tribe, in order to establish friendly relations. Third, they would try to find out what was on the other side of the big lake. Back in their tent that night, Tanama laughed and said, "This must be your last boat trip. Every time you go away, you come back with a new woman. I can't chance that!" Einar laughed quietly.

"But where would I find one like you?" he asked as he

let his hand wander over her body, feeling her move under his hand. Quietly, in order to not wake the children, they explored each other. The next morning as they woke up, he saw Tanama looking at him.

"Something strange happened while you were away," she said, "I dreamt you were in trouble, and that I had to come and help you. But I could not reach you, there were so many strange people crowding around you". He looked at her and told the story of what had happened in the canoe that night.

"It means we belong together, and that your spirit had to help me," he concluded, but it was strange nevertheless. There was much in the spirit world mere humans did not understand.

Red Bobcat was nice to his new woman. He had watched Einar, and realized that kindness often brought good results. He still thought Einar was strange in some regards, not least in the treatment of prisoners, since he knew Einar usually walked away from the ritual killings. Initially Red Bobcat was unhappy with his friend's choice in this regard. To him, the mutilations were necessary at times to keep the enemies spirit from returning. At other times, torture was performed to honor a god. Since Einar had become one of his best friends, he never let Einar know that he believed him to be weak in this regard, and defended him if others in the tribe observed the same. The gods seemed not to mind Einar's absence in any way, as his luck always seemed good. Red Bobcat married the new girl, and had her accepted into the tribe, naming her "Swallow." She became a good wife, despite being ten years his junior, and gave him the children he had longed for.

CHAPTER 12

Acceptance

Red Hair, oldest son of Tanama and Einar, was an extremely handsome young man. He was turning sixteen, which meant that he was an adult, though not fully accepted as such. In many of the surrounding tribe's one was not really considered an adult until in one's twenties, and in some you were not meant to marry before you were in your thirties. Red Hair shivered at the thought. How could anyone wait that long before they became familiar with the "pleasures." Red Hair led a happy life. Because of his unusual hair color, he was the center of attention for many of the young girls, so much so that people would come from other tribes to see him. Life in an Indian village gave a young man, or woman, an almost unlimited amount of freedom, and his parents were of the easygoing sort. It was a trademark of Einar that he never physically disciplined his children or his wife. He yelled sometimes, but never hit them. The rest of the men would sometimes tease him about this, but he never got angry and did not change his ways.

Tanama, by now in her late thirties, was as beautiful as ever in the eyes of Einar, and as happy as could be. She loved her husband and children, and realized how lucky she had been. She still remembered Macu, and knew that except for the luck of the draw their destinies could have been switched. Red Hair had grown up hearing the stories his parents told of their previous lives. He never tired of the tales of the terrible Maya's, the big battles in the land across the big ocean, the trek and many other mysterious happenings. He had already decided that he would leave the tribe for some time and venture about, his thirst for adventure burning in him as it had in his father. The people he most wanted to meet were the ones called the Anasazi, which lived far to the south. The traders told stories about them, and their wonderful cities. He had not yet told his parents about his plans, or asked for permission to leave. He knew they would ask him to stay. However, he was determined, and since his brother and sister had no plans to leave, he knew his parents would be provided for in their older days.

The tribe's new home was nearly ideal. The first

winter had been a shock, colder than anybody could have imagined. The cold wind whipped down from the North Pole, testing the most determined hunter. Over the years, the tribe had become better and better at handling the cold. Einar could only remember one serious instance of frostbite, a middle aged squaw got gangrene after being outside without covering her fingers properly. Einar and Thorfast were familiar with frostbite from Scandinavia, and Thorfast, who was very skillful with the knife, cut off the woman's affected finger. It worked; her life was saved. Unfortunately that was just about the last time the knife had been used. It was too rusty now, and Einar had discarded it. There were also some instances when people froze to death, but they were all exceptions. With the steadily improved skill in preparing clothes that could stand the extremes of winter, there were few days when the tribe was not out and about, the kids playing in the snow, the men hunting and fishing. A particularly skill was ice fishing. After the initial surprise of seeing the lake frozen solid had passed, Einar took some of the men out on the ice. Though only after he had spent considerable time convincing them it was safe. The ice was so thick men could walk on it for several weeks. The fact that you could walk on water, was by itself a wonder to most of his friends. They had seen ice on the rivers back east, but it was usually too thin to walk on safely. With his war club he hacked a hole in the ice and dropped a fish hook made from bones down the hole. After a short while he pulled up a fish, to the general admiration of his companions. Much as the rest of them enjoyed it though, Thorfast and Einar were the only one to continue fishing this way, enjoying the peace and quiet inherent in this pastime.

The tribe was changing also. Intermarrying with other tribes, they were not really Delaware anymore. Over the centuries most tribes in North America would drift from one part of the country to another, as tribes gained and lost power. But these changes often took generations, developing in small steps.

Einar often reflected upon the way his life had turned out. Like many people throughout the ages who move away from their hometown, he could never be 100% satisfied with his new life. Inwardly, however, he accepted that in spite of every misfortune, he had been fortunate. He enjoyed the hunting and free lifestyle he had in his adopted life, he loved his family, and Tanama was his true companion in most things. They could never fully share and understand each others' pasts, but Einar had Leone and Thorfast for that. Unlike Einar, they never longed for their past lives, but still enjoyed talking about it in their older days.

Gunhild had died the previous spring. She woke up in the middle of the night violently sick, and died the following morning when something burst inside her. The Scandinavians had seen similar illnesses in Europe, but for the Indians it seemed like a mysterious disease from the gods. They tried to heal her with herbs and dances, which were helpful in many cases, but useless against a burst appendix. Thorfast missed her terribly, but took comfort in their children. Though the widow of an unlucky hunter (who had been trampled to death by buffaloes the previous year) moved into his teepee, it was clear to all it was more a marriage of convenience than a love arrangement.

Einar had also noted that Scandinavians and Indians alike were by and large remarkably healthy. Since he came to this new land, he could not remember having been sick for one day. Of all the Europeans, the only one to be seriously sick at all was Gunhild, with her burst appendix. By contrast, thirty was old in Europe, and few people lived much beyond that.

'I should be dead by now,' he mused to himself, 'I am in my forties, an old man.' Save for the unavoidable accidents, most of his new friends lived well into their fifties or sixties, some much longer, despite not eating juicy meat from cows or horses. He often wondered why they were so healthy, and thought it was the air or the water. He missed many things, most of all a horse and good sharp knives. The stone and bronze tools were a pain, but unfortunately they were the best they could find.

On one particular day, Einar was hunting with his two sons. As always they found good game, two deer and a squirrel. It was getting late, and being far from the main camp, the three of them found a hideaway for the night and sat down to eat.

"Tell us about your old land," the boys asked as usual, and Einar told of animals you could ride on, of giant ships and cities, wars and strange customs. The two boys listened in wonder, but without really understanding. Like children of all ages, they used their imagination to fill in for missing knowledge, and the stories they would later retell their children about their grandfather's land took on mythical proportions. Together with their mother's stories of Mayan cities and gruesome customs, they wondered what life was like beyond the mountains and fields of home. On this night as Einar finished his stories, Red Hair looked at him and for the first time asked,

"Do you want to go there, father, if you could I mean?" It was the first time anybody had actually asked Einar the question, though he often enough thought about it. He took his time before he answered, thinking it through, remembering the European world with its endless feuds and wars, its diseases, its slavery and general oppression. Looking at his sons fondly he said,

"Not really," he said, looking at his sons. "My home is here now, I am better off than I ever was before."

He meant it, and hoped that this happy state of affairs would continue for the tribe. He had created a weapons revolution with the introduction of the bow and arrow. He hoped that this would make them able to respond to, and come to some agreements with, the Europeans when they arrived. Einar had no way of knowing that the Black Death combined with a deteriorating climate, and the consequential disappearance of the trade route between Scandinavia, Greenland and Vineland, would set back the European onslaught by 500 years. When it finally came, new weapons made the Indians' bows and arrows an anachronism. That, in combination with the Europeans' blind religious faith and new diseases, would lead to the extermination of many Indian tribes and cultures, while others were reduced to mere shadows of what they had been.

But that was all in the future. For now, Einar

marveled quietly at the healthy life he had, and how he and many of his new tribesmen remained active while they grew old, realizing that in Scandinavia he would most likely have been a sick old man, if alive at all.

And so it was, their campfire but a little bright spot in an enormous land, a small speck on the edge of the Great Plains. But next to it, Einar, his family and tribe enjoyed life to the fullest. It was a good life, maybe too good. The riches of the land also limited innovation and development. The tribes that met the Europeans 500 years later had not evolved much from the time of the Northmen, while Europe had changed beyond recognition. And when the two cultures finally clashed, it was clear one thing had never changed; might makes right, for better and, just as often, for worse.

PRINCIPAL SOURCES AND RECOMMENDED READING

Snorre is the natural inspiration for my story, but I have also enjoyed several other interesting books, many of which I would recommend for further reading. This is not by any stretch of the imagination a comprehensive list, but contains some of what I consider the most useful and enjoyable reading:

• *Westward Before Columbus*, by Kåre Prytz, published by Norumbega Books.
• *The Vikings*, by Ian Heath, published by Osprey Publishing.
• *The Fury of the Northmen*, by John Marsden, published by BCA.
• *The Viking Discovery of America: The Excavation of a Norse Settlement in L'Anse Aux Meadows, Newfoundland*, by Helge Ingstad. Checkmark Books

There is an enormous amount of books available about the Indians, many of them excellent. Most deal with the time after Columbus. To me, the outstanding storyteller, albeit of the post Columbus era, is Allan W. Eckert. However, I want to emphasise the following sources in the context of this, pre Columbian, story:

• *Indians in Pennsylvania*, published by Pennsylvania Historical and Museum Commission
• *Aztec and Maya, Life in an ancient civilization*, by Charles Phillips, published by Hermes House.

• *Encyclopedia of Native Tribes of North America*, by Michael Johnson, published by Chartwell Books.
• *Native American Weapons*, by Colin F. Taylor, published by University of Oklahoma Press.

In addition to books and the internet several good historical magazines are published. Many deal wholly or partially with Indian culture. Another excellent source is National Geographic. It devoted most of their May 2000 issue to the Vikings, and the August 2007 issue to the Maya.